14000 and Above

Vikram S. Virulkar

First published in 2017 by

Becomeshakespeare.com
Wordit Content Design & Editing Services Pvt Ltd
Unit - 26, Building A-1, Nr Wadala RTO, Wadala (East),
Mumbai 400037, India
T:+91 8080226699

This is a work of fiction. Names, characters, businesses, places, events and
incidents are either the products of the author's imagination or used in a
fictitious manner. Any resemblance to actual persons, living or dead, or
actual events is purely coincidental.

©
ISBN 978-93-86487-02-5

DEDICATION

To my Parents.

14000 and Above

ACKNOWLEDGMENTS

I would like to thank my parents for their unrelenting support to whatever I have ever done and my friends being the supportive bunch that they always are.
I would also like to thank the Wordit Art Fund and becomeshakespeare.com along with their teams, which helped get this book out available to you readers

PROLOGUE

People are people, they are as bad or good as we are ourselves, look for the bad in someone and you will find it, look for the good in someone and you will have an excuse for unearthing it. Most people have no idea what they are doing and live their lives one day at a time and on the rare occasion plan ahead for some mundane event that they must celebrate with much pomp and grandeur lest they be reminded how mundane their lives have really become. On the other hand, you have the kind of people who know exactly what they are doing or at least they have a fair idea of what they want to do, they set their lives on doing it and some eventually achieve their goals but by far, the biggest mistake people make, is expecting life to have a conclusion or reason in any form. Life is life, it does not need a reason, this "need" or desperation of things to make sense is important to us, but it's quite obvious that we are not often granted such conveniences, neither are they reserved for someone. They are just what they are, maybe someone would call it dumb luck, some would call it divine providence, I prefer to stick with dumb luck, a random occurrence in the universe has more chance of being true than an all-powerful supernatural entity, but that's just how I see the world, you are free to see the world your way, as long as you don't try to force me into looking for your unicorns. As Hawking said, we are just an advanced breed of monkeys on a minor planet of a very average star, never mind the rest of what he said.

14000 and Above

1

Except for the most unusually removed, everyone has at least one great love. It doesn't matter if the story is complete or not, Romeo and Juliet? No that would be one of those clichés. Maybe the grand old man from the park who left his lover in Karachi when he came to India, anyone who has ever lent him an ear has heard that story, or maybe the guy next door who eloped a month back and can't stop bragging about it. Or maybe it is the Watchman, who perhaps spends his entire salary in long distance calls. Quite frankly, I don't know but I can't forget the first time I saw those eyes, she didn't look at me at first, her passing glare caught me. Her eyes held mine and time stopped. Barring my cousins and some friends, I had never really met a girl in my entire life, much less exchanged looks with one.

It's true what they say, your heart skips a beat, the body goes numb and you can't help but stare like a fool. She quickly withdrew her gaze and concentrated on the umbrella which she was holding, I still stood there, looking and acting like a fool. It was raining cats and dogs, the rabid kind and if you are a young lad walking across Marine Drive, who just happened to notice the most beautiful girl in his life, it doesn't register to bother with the umbrella that much. I just kept walking, hoping she would turn back again and catch my wide grin. Only later would my companions decipher my apparent psychotic behaviour of smiling all the way, I didn't want to be caught without a smile, just in case she looked back. To my disappointment and perhaps just a hint of temporary relief, she didn't. Although I was quite confident of another try the next day, luckily I got exactly what I wanted. Before I knew what was happening, a mutual friend took me over and introduced us! It was as simple as that and here I was thinking of all the elaborate ways that I could use to gain her acquaintance. Fortunately, she didn't think much of our ocular encounter which took place just the previous day. To be honest, I

9

don't even think she even remembered it or maybe she did, I don't know. Even if she did at least she didn't make it awkward and the enormous task of meeting her was done quite easily but then again as sure as the world turns, but how can fate be without irony?

Over the next few weeks found myself thinking about her all day long, talking to her all day long, and importantly trying to be with her as long as it as possible and since we had the same classes, we got to being the textbook definition of best friends in almost no time, or the closest type of friends that a boy can be with a girl, although being "friends" was never the idea. I wanted to tell her how I felt about her. I pictured her falling into my arms as I serenaded her with ballads of undying love; I pictured myself like a knight saving his dame from a dragon. While the pages of this fantasy unfolded thanks to my vivid imagination, I slowly discovered, that the longevity of daydreams are strictly limited to the amount of time you spent dreaming about them and the result of daily life is an entirely different matter altogether. The first few days that I hovered around her, made me realise of a Romeo to be, a man better instructed in wooing a woman than I. Surprisingly and to my much to my delight, he left quickly and without much ceremony, leaving her either angry or bitter, which one it was, I am not sure and frankly I was not bothered, my love was safe again. She proclaimed not be in the mood for love any more. Still, I laboured to find a chink in the armour before I made my move, the first time I got the opportunity to speak with her about such things, she dismissed them entirely and told me of another boy, whose advances had been rewarded while mine, it wouldn't be a long shot to say, had been shooed away like a mongrel. Needless to say, my heart broke into a thousand pieces and while I attempted to pick them up, I contemplated why people considered suicide at refusal of love. Soon after, I took a blade and stared at it for 3 hours but I was too much of coward and too much in love with my own existence to carry out the deed, perhaps I should have.

Eventually, things snowballed, a couple of arguments and simple misunderstandings ruined most of our friendship. Good went to bad, bad went to worse and although ambitious salvage efforts were mounted by mutual friends, it didn't work out. I didn't speak to her for a few years and that is how I got my first lesson in life. "**Women, more than circumstance, will make you do stupid things**". The result was disastrous, I failed at everything, went into depression or a state like it for a couple of years but with the passage of time, things got better, life was beautiful again, other women were attractive again and as that happened, I learnt my second lesson, "**You will inevitably repeat the whole thing with another woman**". To those searching for a reason for your rejections, abandon all hope, unless of course she tells you, then there is no argument but otherwise, a woman may reject you on her mood, disinterest in love, attitude, her pre conceived notions of how a man, boyfriend or husband must be, attraction for another man (even an unacknowledged one) her friends advice, or simply because she can say no. Don't bother too much with it, she always has a reason and don't argue, since she will have more to throw at you. Also the whole thing is pretty dicey because apparently some women like be chased. Of course in non-literal terms, I'd hardly imagine that anybody would like being chased but the point is, when you come to the land of women, there is nothing, absolutely nothing you can be sure of, so smile, bring flowers and either wait for them to be accepted or to be thrown back at your face, in either case be happy and go sip your coffee, or tea if you prefer.

So that is what I was doing, sipping coffee and reading the paper at one of the coffee houses, of which there is no shortage in this city. I am disappointed in the coffee, the taste seems more like one of those fast food chains who mix everything and provide you a cheap, albeit fulfilling meal. Having sampled some of the finest coffee blends, this coffee seems so lifeless in comparison; I think that elitist attitude will wear off eventually. Nevertheless it's too early in the day for something stronger and too late for me to look for another place, so I sit patiently turning pages of the in-house newspaper, waiting patiently for her to arrive. The tone of several people featured in the testimonials brings a smile to my face; their supposed love with this coffee house seems like a match made in heaven, if there is such a thing. The company is sure to pick the loudest, most colourful of characters for such spaces, what people won't do for their 15 minutes of fame. I keep looking at the door every time someone walks in, is it anxiousness? I am not sure, it could very well be the fact that it's been over 20 minutes and she hasn't arrived. I finish my first cup and ask for the table to be cleaned and like clockwork, the table is wiped clean of all the water that dripped from the condensation of the cold plastic container that held the coffee.

The door opens once more, I am waiting for it. She pulls of her sunglasses, revealing her Kohl lined eyes, looks for me in the crowd and waves as she comes closer to the table. She walks with confidence rarely looks down, her eyes now fixated on me.
"Traffic", she snarls whilst letting out a smile as she takes her seat across the small circular granite table across from me.
"Do you know how long I have been stuck?"

"Quite a long, frustrating time I am sure, I am sorry you had to endure it, but you know how it is at this time. People want to get home so they can watch their favourite soap while eating dinner and then turning on the news channel to watch people scream at themselves all the time, then ultimately take a shot at the corrupt politicians, while bribing their way out of a traffic violation .Only then can they can go to sleep and repeat this whole thing all over again tomorrow, isn't the world we live in a delightful place? "

Maybe that wasn't how I should have started.

"I can't figure out if you were a pessimist, sadist or a comedian"

"Hmm, how do you know I am not all three?"

"1, you are too jolly to be a pessimist and 2, you wouldn't treat people the way you do if you were a sadist"

"What about the comedian?"

"It's self-answering isn't it? If you really were a good comedian, I would be laughing."

"Ouch! That last one hurt"

"It was supposed to."

Mildly into a laugh now, I choose not to wait till things become stale.

"So how are things at work?"

"Bad, projects aren't working out, as they should, the Boss decides to drop in every hour to make sure his employees are in a "good" working environment and mind set, all he is actually doing is nervously shaking his leg whenever he stops by a cubicle. It barely hides his dread, he thinks that the project won't work and he will end up on the street with his wife and kids, plus his boss keeps dropping in but that guy is not interested in the project, he is only interested in the interns. Man those interns, all they do is stare in the mirror and adjust their dresses and talk on the phone and pass off these looks to the...."

"Please stop!"

"Why? What's?"

"I asked you how your day was, not a rant about interns"

"Do you know why you don't have a Girlfriend" she snaps.

"What? How did that come up? How did we go from Interns seducing bosses to why I don't have a girlfriend? "

"You don't listen to women"

"Sure I do"

"No, A woman will talk about what's on her mind, all you men just can't figure it out, we don't want you to have opinions or address the topic, we just want to say something and have it heard by another human being, that's it."

"Even if it's complete gibberish?"

"Especially if it's complete gibberish! We measure our men by their ability to remain conscious during our marathons, we were born to talk! So we do" she says it while smiling slyly.

"Wow, that's just great, now I am supposed to believe that every woman that ever came into my life, left me because I have a low tolerance level for gibberish?"
I break into the most delicate of smiles, trying to get my point through, but at the same time, trying not to infuriate her.

She looks at me, eyes clenched and probably categorised me into a chauvinist, her stoic transforms into a forced smile of tolerance.

"What kind of coffee are you having?"

"Hazelnut", I reply without a moment's pause, glad the situation has been diffused, she probably will never go out with me again but I am saved the embarrassment of her splashing water over me and then leaving.

"No, as in hot or cold?"

"Hot, but usually leave it too cool down a little before I drink it, so..."

"Good, I'll have one of those"

"OK, just a moment, I'll get that order going and something to eat? These people have some good sandwiches"

"Hmmm, OK, I'll share one with you"

Now, this girl needs to understand, I am not the kind that shares sandwiches but for this time sake, let us share one and leave the rest of the hunger for the time I go back home.

Once the order is given the boy across the counter gives me a laminated sheet with the number 7 written on it, he smiles broadly and says, "Thank you for your order, it will take 10 minutes and someone will serve you the order on your table, just keep this sheet there" his enthusiasm in thanking me for my order makes me smile, I return to the table to find her talking on the phone, I place the sheet on the table and wait for her to finish her conversation, which seems pretty damn long, few minutes later, and she signals to me that she will be done shortly, I wave my hand and move my lips to say no problem without a sound. Those Kohl eyes are just too beautiful, it's difficult to look away but before she finds me staring at her, I look around the floor, the place is quite full today. Plenty of people, coming here to pass their time, no one can put it any differently, what amuses me the most is the two seemingly professional businessmen, who have their laptops out and have ordered coffee that they haven't touched and both are on the mobile phone to some other people, well, that's progress for you. Also sitting nearby are these college kids, loud and unrefined, I suppose let them be, it's the last time they think that they have their freedom, before it is burdened by looking for Jobs to make a living. The phone rings, damn! It's the Psycho again; I disconnect her call in a hurry. By this point she finally gets off the phone and all I do is smile at her. She breaks the pause again and starts speaking normally. Not a moment too soon.

"That was my colleague from office; we are moving to phase 2 of our project tomorrow"

"I thought you said the project wasn't going that well?"
"Yeah, but some bugs were rectified today after I left and the next phase has got the green light"

"You don't seem too happy about it."

"I have been working so hard, so long, I just don't know what I am working for any more, it's always deadline this, Client agreement that, I don't want to do this anymore.

"So quit."

"I hate my job but I love my pay check."

I laugh a little and this time she joins me.

Our coffee & food arrives, and not a minute to late, I lunge for the sandwich as does she; I am guessing she is pretty hungry but doesn't want to come across as such. Trying to be polite, as far as initial meetings go.

"Another Sandwich?" I offer just as we finish our first one in less than 10 minutes.

"Maybe; but after the coffee"

"Cool"

We spend the next hour talking about inconsequential things, or simply said we engage in small talk, and then we shift to our friends and how they are doing. We end up ordering another sandwich and have some laughs too. It's quite interesting when you find yourself talking to someone and forgetting what you did and what you are going to go and just live in the moment. That's what both of us were doing. We had let everything go and were just enjoying each other's company. That is, before she looked at the clock.

"I have to leave; need to catch the local back home"

"So soon? Can't we stay a little longer?" I say, trying to cajole her.

"No, please, my aunties would miss me", she laughs, refereeing to the group of train friends who share the compartment, lots of those in Mumbai, just friends for the journey.

"OK, I am going to hang around a bit more, take a walk maybe."

"Hey, free this Sunday? Maybe, we could go watch a movie and have some dinner before we go home"

"Uhh...OK, I suppose that's a good idea, why don't I text you by tonight?"

"Sure, let me know, Bye"

Just like that, she left, I could hardly believe my luck, we had a good time, she likes what I say, I don't find her drab and of course, the whole 'text you by night thing' was just something you say not to sound desperate, of course it's a yes! I'd have to be certifiably mad to say no to that.

I pay my bill, and walk out to Marine Drive, I feel the salty mist that is in the air as the waves crash against the rocks and concrete barriers. I hadn't felt so good in years; I look at the sea, close my eyes, smile and take a deep breath.

2

Groggy and hung over, that's how I feel, probably would have felt better if I did have some alcohol. After 2 days of travelling in this weather, this whole place seems like shit to me, and of course, the highly paid pilots want a better deal, so please cancel our flights and let us rot in places like this. Everything is bad here, the weather, the wind, the cold, I hate the cold. Out in the distance, a board almost buried by the mud. It reads "CHU" the first three letters covered by mud from the flows, the last three I think describes this place better. Does it even make sense to have something this far up? Every breath I take seems like an effort and since the driver had the good sense to drive so long so fast, We had to stay in this place, which seems like a badly shot episode of Survivor. Out on the roads I can't see anything or anyone, whatever happened to the air conditioning and heaters?

 He pondered over his situation and took deep mouthfuls of the soup, the soup wasn't high on taste but at least it was hot, it was difficult to pass up something hot here. He curled up his toes and rubbed them for a minute. Just five hours ago, he was getting out of the car, getting his feet wet in the freezing waters which were running off the glaciers, stepping into the waters and throwing stones into the holes, just to make a makeshift bridge so, that the car could go through and not sink into the holes, how he remembered the crow and the bottle story then. He couldn't afford to get his shoes wet, that would have been really bad, and so he ventured with the drivers slippers. His feet went numb by just staying in the stream, so did his hands after he handled the cold stones. His right hands thumb was still giving him some pain; he clasped the soup bowl, trying to get some heat off it. He remembered why he was here and looked towards the centre of the camp where now a bonfire was burning, slowly as darkness descended into the valley, the white tents glowed golden with the ambient light of the fire, it was still cold and dry. The driver sat near the fire, brought out a cigarette and lit it with a stick from within the fire, he didn't understand the frustration of his passenger, most people loved it out here, the wide open spaces and the loss of things that people find mundane, this one was obviously different, with a yawn, he flung the butt into the fire and went inside his tent to sleep peacefully.

Our man had more on his mind than usual; he looked over the files again and again. Trying to spot errors or any miscalculations, he went through the proposal, making sure it was optimized for the presentation. It wasn't an easy night for him, within 4 days he had been uprooted from his cosy Bangalore office and made to travel more than 3,000 kilometres to this shithole, travelling ticket less in trains, to riding on the roof of a bus, to finally hiring a car to take him to the road to heaven, his eyes started drooping slowly and after 2 hours of shuffling through files and starting into his laptop, he was finally asleep.

 A voice wakes him up early next morning, urging him to wake up but he is too tired and sleepy to bother

"Sir, we have to go now, or else it will be late"

"What? Why did you come inside? Go, I want to sleep for some time now"

"No sir, sleep in the Car if you want, we cannot wait any more, its already 6:30."

"What???? You woke me up at 6:30??? Go, go away now, let me sleep, come back after three hours"

"No sir, we must go now, it snowed a little last night, the roads must be slippery and we should go before sun melts the Ice and makes the road dangerous"

"Fine, whatever, I am coming, now can you please go out so i can dress up and go to the bathroom?"

"Yes Sir, but the bathroom is outside,"

"Yes, I know that, thank you, thank you for reminding me"

Half an hour later, as he made his way to the car, he was feeling a little better, the chill was still there but he was breathing a little easily now, A product of getting some rest he thought. He slipped inside the car with his laptop and files and tried to sleep but it was simply impossible with the sun shining on his eyes or the constant rocking of the car and since there are more potholes in the road that there is an actual road. He gave up the idea and sat through the journey. Majestic mountains enamoured with white crowns of show seemed close enough to touch, glaciers rode out to the meet roads, and the place was tranquil, as if no human had ever come through here, the silence was deafening as well as disturbing, the simple isolation of the place was beyond belief. The only sound was the sound from the engine of the car.

"First time in Ladakh Sir?" Asked the driver trying to talk his way out of boredom.

"Yes"

"Didn't bring your wife?"

"No, I'm not married."

"Oh, why not ? , Sir you are handsome man, a good educated man too, you will get a good girl, I have been married 9 years, I have 2 Kids, both of them go to school, I will make them like you sir, Good educated Gentlemen. "

"I'm happy to know that" he said while smirking a little, frankly, he was the only company he had in the last 4 days.

"You are from here? From Manali?" He asks his driver

"No sir, I am from a small Village in Zanskar, but now I Work in

Manali, In our village, we don't have any work at this time? We come down to help the tourists."

"So your family stays with you in Manali or they stay in the village??" he asks

This time he didn't reply, he was staring at some clouds moving in.

"Close your windows Sir, it will get very cold" He says quite abruptly, I don't complain, it was getting to be quite chilly, we are beginning to climb steeply, the view is getting more foggy and finally, we encounter it, snowfall, it's the first time I see snow falling down from the skies, I have only seen rain, never experienced this, for the first time in those dreaded days, I get into happier, less dreary state, I roll down my window and stick my hand outside, and feel the snowflakes, it's a strange feeling, almost as lighter than a feather, it looks like small pieces of cotton falling from the skies, I bring my hand inside to analyse the snow, in about a minute, its melted and only some cold water in my palms remains. "Should have bought some warm clothes", I think aloud to myself, my driver is unusually quiet; he had been in the chatty mood for the couple of hours, what seems to have silenced him? I prod him a few times even try to crack a bad joke, it doesn't take his attention off the road and the skies, he simply nods and looks further onto the road. I always thought about how I would react if I ever encountered snow, I fantasied about creating snowballs and hurtling them at people, making snow angels and just living out boyish fantasies, this is certainly not the idea I had in mind. Visibility is getting worse and that entire good mood vanishes. My driver is spooked and seeing my driver in that mood spooks me even more. We reach a point where the road doesn't seem so bad and it's a flat relatively straight stretch.

He stops the car, gets out and walks to a Stone marker, I realise we are at Taglang la pass, apparently the second highest motor able pass in the world. I see him kneeling down in the front of the prayer flags and uttering something, perhaps a prayer. How can he be out in weather like this? It had to be below 0 outside. Quickly the snowfall increases without warning and I find myself thinking, if I should join him. Wouldn't hurt, would it? I step outside the car, its bone chilling and as I make my walk to the marker, I feel mouth getting dry, breathing again, becomes harder, well. What am I to expect at more than 17,000 feet? I drop to my knees beside him, fold my hands and start saying a prayer quietly. Quietly wishing for this ordeal to be over.

The driver gets up and looks amazed that the man prayed right beside him,

"I didn't take you for the praying type."

"Well, God is always with you, sometimes we need to remind him that we are with him too and looking at the weather, I needed to tell him that I remember him now."

"Very good sir, should we continue now?"

We pull away from the curve and start down now, the climate hasn't changed and the chill is getting worse. As I thought, we didn't spot anyone on the road, it was unusually isolated. As my driver comes up a bend, he asks me to look to my left, he asks me to look into the distance where he says three cars fell off the road in the last week, I can't see it, so he points, and just he points, out from the curve comes a Large Army truck headed straight for us, the road is too small, there is no place to swerve its either the truck or the valley, "Oh God!"

3

"I am told that waiting for a woman before marriage is bliss and after marriage a sorrowful duty."

"Yes, you would know wouldn't you?"

"Yes, I am the only one you know, who knows actually, In my case, waiting for her lawyer to serve me my divorce papers was he only bliss I ever got."

"I don't get you, you marry in a rush, you rent a house, and after a year, you're calling it quits?"

"We made a mistake, we weren't right for each other. We rushed it, how many times are we going to go over this?"

"Hey, you brought the divorce up, I didn't"

"Sorry, forget about it Hey! How did your date go?"

"Well, I wouldn't go so far as to calling it a Date. We had a good time, we talked, we drank coffee and then left, although what we are having this Sunday is most definitely a date!"

"Well done my man! Tell me how does she look?"

"She has the most beautiful eyes and that Kohl, oh, that Kohl, it makes me want to look into her eyes all day long, she is slim, a little dark in complexion, she has an amazing smile, although her teeth stick out a little bit, she has got a good sense of humour and well, I just like her. "

"Sounds amazing, I wish I could meet her."

"Well, get in line, plus aren't you recently divorced? Shouldn't you be playing out the emotionally unavailable stereotype at the moment?

We both laugh it off, as our server brings in two pints and we put them together for a toast to chasing women who tend to run away from us. The rest of the evening is spent in similar unproductive talks and finally by 9, we decide we have had too much and leave the Pub and hail a Cab for the station. I manage to flag one down and gently hold his arm to make him sit inside the cab. We reach the Station and after I pay the Cabbie, it's time to Board a train out of here. He takes my arm and we manage a window seat in a slow train, he loves the window seat, although it might be noted, very few don't like it. In fact I am surprised, why, in Mumbai, nobody has started a black market for window seats in local trains. The train leaves and the slow movement of the train makes him fall asleep, let him. He probably had one more than he should have. At least he is not throwing up. I pull out my phone to check if I missed something, an e-mail by some generous fellow who wishes to share his winnings from the great American lottery, what's more if I just send him my bank account number, he will put all of 3 million Dollars into my account, so generous of him. The phone rings just as I hit the delete button, and as luck would have it, Shanaya's call is accidentally answered. I know this conversation is going to be awkward, although, I am hoping that after a few awkward conversations, she might lose interest but well, you know what they say about a man's luck, you never seem to have it, when you need it the most.

"Too busy you have become!"

"Too much work, I am sorry"

"It's ok, so what's up? Are you coming by?" She asks this almost every time.

"No, not today, it won't be possible; I am still out for work"

"What's this?? Every time you do this, today you have to come and meet me. "

"Hello...Hello, hey can you hear me???"

"Yes, I can hear you, Vivek "

"Hello... Hello"
And just like that, I disconnected my phone. The "in the train" excuse never fails.

The P.A system in the train announces the arrival of the most mysterious place on the planet. Of course, its Dadar, The nonsense capital of Mumbai. Now there is a precise Math to this, the number of people who will Board at Dadar is inversely proportional to the strength of your desire to go home quietly and without feeling stampeded over by a herd of wild buffaloes. The more you wish it would be quiet and happy, the more people would barge in. Forget the Math; people will barge in for no rhyme or reason, where do these people go? Where do they come from? Do they even have real jobs? Or are they just paid to make our lives miserable, by climbing in and out of Dadar Station. I look over at Arun, he is sound asleep, for next time, I'll make a mental note to drink in excess and pass out on the train so it won't be that frustrating. My phone beeps, it's her
"

Had a great time today,
Thanks for the coffee and your company,
Looking forward to Sunday :)
"

Wow! She likes me! I think to myself, my mood lifts and I don't mind the crowd anymore and a slight smile remains plastered to my face. As soon as we reach our destination, I wake up Arun and grab his arm; I slowly walk him out of the doors and into a Rick. After a quick ride, we arrive at his house. Although drunk, he reminds me several times of his sobriety, urging me to home and not drop him off. When I persist and when he makes a final request for another beer, I oblige. Since he is going home, there certainly isn't any harm, the worst that can happen is that he can shout all night and wake the neighbours. An acceptable risk. I buy four from a Wine Shop and get back into the rick. We reach his home and as I ask for the keys to open the door, I realise Arun is visibly upset about something. I open the door, he walks in and stumbles at the table and crashes on the couch. I visit the Wash room and quickly freshen up before joining Arun. As I am back, Arun is already fondling the Can and waiting for me to open mine. I oblige and raise the can customarily.

"To getting drunk and finding no one at home to bother you about it"

No sooner did we toast, I noticed a tear running down his eye, I inquired instantly.

"Arun, what's wrong?"

"Shit man! What was her problem?"

"You're talking about your wife again, aren't you?" I asked leaning back into the couch.

"Who else do you think I would talk about?"

"This has gone on long enough, it has to stop and you have to accept that she is gone."

"It's me isn't it? Who wants to be married to a guy who can't even tell her how beautiful she looks"

"It's not like that, you two have other problems, you have to see it from .."

"I can't fucking see!" He roared as he cut me halfway, tossing his can in the air, it flew by my shoulder as it hit the ground and foam started spilling out on to the floor.

"I'm sorry, please, I'm sorry, I don't know what happened."

"I do, I know exactly what happened, and you're drunk. Now, I am telling you as a friend, I love you like a brother but I am not your babysitter. You have to stop feeling sorry for yourself. Whatever happened, happened, it wouldn't have happened any other way, be glad that this is over, or you are just going to be some blind, drunk homeless man on the streets, do you get me? We all have to play the hand we have been dealt, you just have to do the best with what you have"

That was it, the moment he stopped drinking and started crying, what did he do wrong? Nothing, he was just married the wrong woman. 2 years ago, people would listen to his stories to be inspired, a blind man passing out with flying colours from the IIM. Recruited instantly by a top Finance company and despite his handicap, doing extremely well. Indians have a problem when it comes to marriage; our parents get jumpy when their kids cross 25. Arranged marriages are often the norm and mostly, kids are expected to compromise and make the forced relation work, Radha wasn't a bad girl, an average looking girl, with a good personality. Her parents thought "So what if the man is blind, he makes a 7 figure salary". Arun's parents thought, "What? Our blind son will be married? What are we waiting for?" We all sensed some problems when he first introduced her to us, she wasn't happy, Arun was ecstatic though, he thought he was finally going to have a normal life. Things didn't go as smooth and Radha left him around 8 months later, after months of bitter fighting.

 I didn't get involved too much, only after I got word that she was planning to leave him, I intervened. She didn't want to get married to a blind man, didn't want to care for him, or "Carry him around like baby" as she put it. She didn't want this life for her, her parents begged her to reconsider for the sake for their "names", what face
Would they show to the rest of the world? She didn't bother. Arun made some nasty comments about her at the time of leaving; he was unfortunately, madly in love with her to let her go. The loneliness was killing him, the thought of not having Radha around maddened him, and he hit the bottle and remained drunk whenever he found it convenient. He still imagined the time when Radha was with her, however brief that moment. I kept track of Radha, now and then

calling her, listening to what she had to say about Arun and how she thought he wasn't a bad guy. "It just won't work out" she said, "I need someone normal" she repeated many times, in many conversations. I gave up after a month, this girl wasn't coming back. Last I heard, she was seeing a gym instructor. I didn't tell Arun, it would just depress him more.

He stops crying and asks for some alcohol, which I obviously don't give him. He too drunk anyway, I carry him to his bed where crashes in an instant.. I take his phone, set an alarm for 7:00 and walk out the apartment.

I hail a Rick and get in, as I make my way home; I remove my phone from my jeans to see if someone missed me,

"4 missed Calls- Mom"

Someone did miss me. My mother, being a mother, dialled my number 4 times in a row, since I wasn't picking up, it wouldn't have occurred to her, that I would be busy or stuck somewhere or just not able to pick up the phone. No, surely those things must not occur to mothers, they must speak to their children in any circumstance, a smile escapes my lips and I call her to face the music.

"Hello, I have been trying so long and so hard to reach you are all right?"

"Yes Ma, I am fine, the phone was on silent so I didn't hear it."

"But you should at least check and call"

"Yes, I am sorry; I'll to take the first call next time"

"Good, did you have your dinner or should I heat some up for you?"

"No, I had my dinner; I will be home in some time"

"OK, come quick, its late now".

Ricks are becoming too expensive, I think to myself as I see the meter running to break some record, it's after midnight now and the night charge seems determined to bankrupt me. I finally reach home and after unhappily paying the driver, I open the door and carefully remove my shoes, so as not to wake Dad up. I don't bother tip toeing around the Bedroom, I know Mom's awake, she won't sleep until she makes sure that her only son is safe, and more importantly fed properly.

I take a mattress out, put on my bed sheet and pillows and lie down after a long day, I close my eyes to try and fall asleep and before slipping into a deep sleep, all I see are those beautiful Kohl eyes.

4

Another delay, just my luck, guess I am lucky.

He sits near the bend, the same bend where he could have lost his life just moments ago, a twist of luck and 10 inch piece of sharp metal pierced one of the tyres and making the car swerve to the right, into the mountain. The Car was safe and the driver of the Army truck braked just in time. It could have gone any other way, it didn't. He gets up from the bend; his legs are still shaking from the adrenaline. He opens his case, lights a cigarette looks into the valley. "Sure is a very long way down". It's still very cold but the fog is lifting. He makes out a figure dressed in Army fatigues walking over to him. He looks over at him and gestures for a cigarette, although he is running low on them, he gives the man one, lights it and the two stand on the edge of the bend.

"Beautiful isn't it?"

"I beg your pardon?"

"I said, it's quite beautiful, the view from up here, I saw you looking out."

"Oh that, I was just contemplating how many turns the car would take, before it exploded into a fireball,"

"Of course, you have seen too many movies", he says letting out a smile

"Yes, the thought does get to you when you just escaped a situation like this."

"Where are you headed?"

"Leh, was hoping to get there before nightfall"

"Don't worry, you'll make it, the roads are pretty much sorted from here on. Care for some tea? We are stopping here for a while, to run checks and rest a little."

"Thank you, that would be wonderful, my driver would love some if you can spare it"

"Of course, I'm Shakeel Ali" he says, with a outstretched hand,

"It's a Pleasure Captain, My name is Arjun Joshi" I reply with a firm handshake.

"You know the ranks; do you have a forces background?"

"No, my parents retired last year after 30 years in a Bank but I think everyone in the country ought to know a bit about the men and women protecting their soil. Knowing how to read ranks from shoulder badges certainly wouldn't hurt."

"Absolutely, civilians should know a bit about their Army, maybe that would motivate them to join, it's a good, honest profession, filled with honour and respect that you get for a lifetime. It's disappointing to know that we are facing a shortage of officers"

"True" he says, as he takes the hot mug from another Soldier, while he is waiting to take the first sip, Capt. Ali sends the driver another mug.

"So, what brings you to these desolate hills? Can't be national security?" He laughs while gulping down some of the tea.

"No, actually I am here on an official trip, My company makes some unique products that we think would interest some buyers here, personally, I think this trip could have come at a better time, the weather is just something else up here."

"Been posted here for 3 years now, never seen weather like this, It's almost unbelievable, it's never this cold this time of the year, we almost never have snowfall or roads jammed with snow at this point."

We go back and forth about some things, with Capt. Ali giving me some advice about the people and terrain and more importantly, the weather. We finish our cup of tea and by that time, the driver has finished replacing the tyre and the Army Caravan is also ready to move.

"Thank you Sir, for the tea as well as some of the help, the Army has been most helpful where ever we have gone."

"Our pleasure Arjun. Take care."

With that good bye, we get back into our car, and head back on to Leh.

True to every last detail, the road to Leh was very good; we made up for lost time and reached just before 7 P.M. I checked into a Hotel and gave my driver a room to stay. I called the Reception to see if they would be able to make a long distance call for me, after they told me the rates, I decided it would be better to call from a phone booth outside. I ventured out, even though I didn't want to, my legs were cramped from all that travelling and I had a splitting headache from the trip to Leh. I spot a place where there are private phone booths. I get into one and dial my boss.

"Sir, it's me, Arjun"

"Where the hell have you been? Do you realise that you haven't checked in two days? We were about to inform the Police"

"I'm sorry Sir, it seems that in this state prepaid numbers from the outside are blocked and getting hold of a phone was really tough."

"Well, where are you now?"

"In Leh Sir, according to schedule"

"Have you spoken with Colonel Brar or someone from his office?"

"No sir, I will make the call tomorrow, it's too late now. I just arrived"

"No Arjun! You were supposed to make the call today and meet him tomorrow."

"Unfortunately Sir, there was a little delay, the car met with an accident and we lost some time there"

"Accident? Are the pass keys OK?"

"Yes, they are fine sir," I flinch as I am surprised that he is only concerned with the bloody package.

"Listen Arjun, I know this job is a tough one, that's why I have assigned it to you, you told me that you wanted to work in a challenging environment where your skills are utilized. This is your chance, if you do well, I will make sure the company sees what a great asset you are and well, maybe you bump up a few positions and drive around in a Merc. If you don't deliver, we could have some serious problems, do you understand?"

"Yes Sir I do. Thank you for letting me know, Goodnight Sir."

What a prick!, I think to myself as pay the booth operator. The walk back to the Hotel is much longer than I made the first time. Challenging environment where my skills are utilized? What the hell was I thinking? I don't even remember I said that! That's only babble that people say during interviews, no one really means that! I blankly watch the market, look at the uniquely Ladakhi design, scamper through the old market and see prayer flags up for display, people turning prayer wheels and bargaining with tourists. I reach my hotel, open my room and slip silently into the covers. This is a good bed. I like this bed.

5

I don't particularly like Sundays, it is to me as any other day, I love the free time I get, but most Sundays are full of mundane things that bore me to no end. I trust, this Sunday would be entirely different. I have a date planned with a beautiful woman and nothing could get me away from that. Or at least such is the idea. I must be on guard, my friends rarely all group together these days, and when they do, they will try all the things possible to get me away from my elaborate plans and try to persuade me into joining their exploits, funny how that works, especially when they have active romantic lives. They seem to want to leave their better halves behind and embark on a "boy's trip". It truly is ridiculous how they tip toe around the whole thing. While all they want, is to get away from their wives, girlfriends and other women who don't yet have a formal designation. What was interesting to note, that when I declined to come along for this affair, they were stunned into silence, perhaps from the past record of me not having a single date in recorded history.

History, in this context is defined by the period ranging from the current day to exactly 730 days before, or 2 years, 731 in case it is a Leap year, anything from before doesn't count, although I didn't have anything to boast about in pre-history either. So here was the dilemma, my friends wanted me to come away to some place where the women didn't show and I wanted to be with a woman who, I was quite confident was the best thing that happened to me in history. I have to admit, we went to some amazing places in our trips. The experience was exiting and worth repeating many times over but this time I was not going to rule in favour of the majority.

Fortunately for me, I didn't have to make that decision. Late, on Saturday evening, I got a call from one of my friends, who called in to cancel the trip; his wife was cross with him for going alone and wanted to come along. Apparently this Sunday, a trip to her mother's wasn't going to cut it for her and as luck would have it, another friend called to say he wasn't going make it, his girlfriend's friends, cancelled their plans of going out. So he was stuck with her, that's how he put it. Now men are simple creatures, we like the simple things in life; although we may seem sophisticated at times but on the inside we really are 5 year old kids who want to random things because they can be done. These Sunday trips were the perfect escape for us, to escape into fantasy land and live out our desire to go where we want, eat what we want, drink what we want and ogle at beautiful women without having to worry about a set of eyes burning into the back of our heads. This was a disaster for my friends, but they stuck up another idea, what if, we could all go on the trip and have me bring my date along?

For them, it was a brilliant idea, a change in plan; they could bring their better halves along, yet, would not miss out on the fun of going on a trip! Unfortunately for me, I did not want to go through the trauma, of having my buddies along with me. Telling every embarrassing detail about my life to my date, here I run into a problem again, back to square one. I can't blow off my friends and I definitely will not blow off my date. Although, if I ask her to go out with me on a trip, she might think I have the wrong idea but such is life, you blackmail your friends and most times, they blackmail you too.
So, I make the call scared and not knowing the outcome.

"Hey Riya, how are you?"

"Hey! I'm good, how are you?"

"I'm OK, I hope I didn't catch you at a bad time, I can call later if..."

"Please, I think we know each other enough to get formalities out of the way."
I laugh, it's a superficial one and she sees through it.

"So, what's up? I'm really looking forward to tomorrow. I have already picked this fantastic movie and also planned out the café"

"Yes, about that, I called in to ask you if we could make a change in that plan"

"What sort of change?" Her voice, now drooping and inquisitive.

"Well, I was thinking, remember how I told you about the trips that we guys take? This time it's their wives and girlfriends who coming along with us too. So maybe you can also come in for the trip?"

"As your girlfriend?" Her voice is now stern and all I can imagine is that she is seething with anger, this friend blackmailing thing? It's turning out to be ugly

"No, absolutely not, not as my girlfriend, it would" I counter, although before I can complete my sentence, another sentence comes out, the knockout punch.

"So, you don't want me to come as your girlfriend and your friends and their wives very well know that you not married and you are asking me to come out on a trip with you without them knowing what kind of relationship we share? What kind of girl would I be made out be? Vivek, what kind of a girl do you think I am? " she says this flatly, without any hint of emotion or rage, this is what frightens me even more.

She has stunned me into silence; I dare not utter a single syllable for fear of invoking her wrath. I am unsure of what to say and there is silence on the phone for almost 15 seconds but it seems like eternity. All that is now registering in the mind is to disconnect the call.

Before I can move my thumb to the phone, I hear a slight giggle.

"Boom that just happened, I turned the motor mouth into a silent movie"

"What?"

"Please, you think, you can be the only one pulling jokes around here?"

"What the hell Riya! You almost gave me a heart attack"

"Oh really? Learn to take a joke, you'll live longer."

"Yes, yes, very funny, all right?"

"Actually, I wouldn't mind taking some time to visit some places around the city, never really been outside except for the vacation trips to the native place."

"So, you'll come?"

"As long as we are back by 10."

"Sure we will, I mean we will try our best" I snicker a little.

"No wait, I am getting second thoughts" she says doing a little snickering of her own, this girl is fast, and she obviously knows she has me by the leash

"No, I assure you, we will be back by 10"

"That's better, what time should I be ready?"

"Say, around 9 or 9:30 maybe?"

"OK, cool goodnight then, catch you in the morning."

"Goodnight"

I can't believe that worked, I call up my friends and give them the news, they are happy that the plan worked and it's a win-win for everybody, I end the conference with a bit of caution to both of them, letting them know, that if their better halves like the trip, this could very well be a weekly affair for them, the girls might want to come every Sunday. There is a moment of horrified silence as they imagine the possible repercussions. They were so busy planning about how to keep the women happy for the next day; they failed to see the larger picture. I laugh and disconnect the phone

Isn't the whole idea of being with someone by definition mean that you will be with that someone? I know, that being with the wrong person, or being madly in love with someone, who doesn't love you back, hurts like no other pain can. It rattles your very foundation, makes you want to curl up in a corner and shut the world out, I know, I've been there. What surprises me sometimes is that, when these people have love, why do they reject it? Surely there must be something wrong with them, or is it?

6

The day has just begun, fortunately, there is a lot less grogginess today, more of a relaxed feeling, almost peaceful, I haven't felt so peaceful in years, I wake up pleasantly and look out the window for some time, people go about their way, there is a chill in the weather, it must have snowed last night, there is still some snow on my window, this weather really is weird, almost unheard of. Snow in September. I light up a cigarette and switch on the T.V, news of how the weather is doing keeps flashing, the Manali-Leh highway is now closed, people who have made it this far, are blocked in. Thank God I got here in time; I take a quick breakfast of an Omelette and some orange juice and make my way off to the phone booth I went to last night. I get in the booth and dial a number for the Army acquisitions centre in New Delhi.

"Good Morning, how may I help you?"

"Good Morning, May I speak to Colonel Brar's office in acquisitions?"

"Who may I say is calling?"

"This is Joshi from Accurate Technologies."

"Hold 2 minutes please."

"Yes, thank you."

The hold time is strange, there is no music, that's odd, most places, there is at least a single chime, here there is only a beep to remind you that, you have not been disconnected.

"Hello, who is this?"

"Good Morning, this is Arjun Joshi, from Accurate Technologies, may I speak with Colonel Brar?"

"Yes Joshi, I wasn't really expecting your call, I thought all the roads have been closed from to Leh"

"Well Sir, I made it before I got snowed in."

"Good, are you ready?"

"Yes Sir, If you could just tell me how to..."

"Come in at 1300 Hrs. to the Army hall of fame and then leave your car behind, show your visiting card and ID at the registration counter and they will make arrangements for your transportation to the location of the test."

"Sure Sir, who must I speak to once I get there?"

"Why me, of course."

"Oh, I thought you were in New Delhi, since I called there"

"Don't be naive, you know that calls can be transferred anywhere, you work in an office, don't you?"

"Sure Sir. No problem will be there."

"Good, Anything else?"

"No Sir, that's all"

"Very well, see you at the meeting"

As soon as he said that, he put down the receiver, I was about to say Goodbye. Apparently, the Colonel wasn't.

I moved on quickly back to the Hotel and got my driver along with me. I asked him to wait at the reception while I quickly went upstairs and took a quick bath and put all my things together. Within half an hour, I made it back to the lobby and asked the driver to take me to the Army hall of fame. The Army hall of fame is a museum made to honour the armed forces that valiantly protect the country with all they can; laying down their lives if necessary to make sure that their country is always safe. As is my nature, I made it to the place just in time for 1 P.M. I walked hurriedly to the registration centre and presented him with my visiting card and ID, the soldier took his time, looking at documents and then looking at me, at 3 or 4 hard stares. He then asked me to wait inside for 5 minutes.

I went inside the Museum and looked upon the exhibits while I waited for the Soldier to return with a car. This place was filled with things I only heard off but never thought I would see up close. Things like the personal memorabilia of Pakistani Soldiers, which was found during the Kargil War of 1999. Other things like Identity cards, one of a Major and some Subhedars. Pay books, Music CD's, books and lots of personal correspondence between the Soldiers and their families some of it collected from the dead soldiers and some of it collected after their bunkers were captured. Big photographs adorned the walls of the Museum of soldiers waving the Tricolour above mountain peaks, which were re captured after the war. Below the photographs were representations of how each battle was won, a POP model painted black and showing the advance of different regiments on the peaks of the occupied mountains. The guns and artillery didn't interest me very much; I had already seen them all. There was a Siachen exhibit that caught my eye and as soon as I started walking towards it, the soldier called out my name. I promptly came up and was expecting a car waiting for me, only there wasn't a car, there was a truck.

"You can't be serious" I said to the soldier who had escorted me and was now gesturing towards the truck.

"Yes Sir, you will board this truck and get to the location as discussed"

"No, you see I need a car, since I will be carrying some equipment along with me"

"Plenty of space in the truck."

"Yes, but."

"Those are my orders, to escort you to the truck, now if you would excuse me, I have other things to take care of."

He got the feeling that the rest of the journey was just about as bad as getting here; he didn't like the idea all that much.

7

I love the Sea, Being born here, in Mumbai, it's quite impossible for any resident of Mumbai or "Mumbaikar" not to love the Sea, Mumbai Is after all an Island. I grew up in a time when Mumbai was called Bombay, a remnant of the British era, funnily the British never gave it that name, the Portuguese are responsible for that, from the derivation of the Word Bom Bhaiya, which means Good Harbour. The Portuguese controlled Bombay for some period of time, before it was offered as dowry to the British in a Royal Wedding. The British knew Bombay was a good harbour and very happy to have received such a present, maybe it was them who requested it. From there the name was anglicised to Bombay and the British were here to stay. Bombay then, looked nothing like it did now, a quick look into the maps of the old, will give one a very different view from the Mumbai of today. Although, through reclaiming of the land thought the years, the Islands were interconnected and the British set out to develop Bombay as one of the hubs of the country, and very soon, it gained a seat of power, and eventually eclipsing Calcutta, now Kolkata as the major economic city of India during the Colonial period. Once the English were gone and all Indians were free from the Raj, Mumbai, still continued to be the financial Capital of the Country with a ridiculous amount of money which changes hands everyday in the city   if   dreams.

 it's impossible for a Mumbai to stop speaking about the charm of the City with many names, The Island City, the City of dreams or perhaps the most apt, the City that never sleeps, speaking of which, I still haven't managed to sleep. Its chronic Insomnia, resulting from years of Night Shifts as a Call Centre executive for British and American Companies. Its almost 5 and all I have got is around two hours' worth of sleep, I think it's no point trying anymore and I get up and read a book, I make sure I read it in the Kitchen, so as, not to wake up my parents.

I can't help but keep getting these feelings of fulfilment and joy as I sit of the cold floor reading the book, my mind already preoccupied with Riya and her eyes. It's no use, i try to keep imagining them, like some star struck teenager. I get up and fix myself a butter and sugar sandwich, it's one of my favourite things, nothing simpler than two slices of bread, butter on them and sugar sprinkled on one side. I make sure it's not that horrid salt free butter that mom brought in, Indians, usually have a very highly developed taste for salted butter, usually the appearance of butter is white, but we have always seen our butter as yellow, a side effect of the addition of salt. After eating it for years, we quite like our butter; we normally detest unsalted butter, even though it may be healthier. Indian food though is a paradox, there aren't a lot of options if healthy food is on your mind, tasty and fulfilling is what does the trick for us. As I finish my snack, I feel sleep coming over me and eventually make it back to the bed.

I wake up, abruptly by noise of a political march happening outside, it feels as if I had just gone to sleep, I check my phone, its almost 11. I haven't been able to sleep well. I haven't had good night's sleep in years. I drag myself out of bed and make it to the living room, where Dad is reading the paper. I pick up a stray page lying nearby.

Freak weather hits North India, Snow Storms expected in J & K, Uttaranchal and Himachal Pradesh."

8

The Sights which I saw so often on my way to get here, elude me now, all I can see from the inside of this green painted metal can are the faces of two soldiers who seem to be instructed not to talk to me, the reason that they seem so distant is not so obvious. They don't seem like regular soldiers, unless they come armed to the teeth with grenades, two extra mags and a 9mm. The usual issue is just the INSAS.

"Pretty cold day" I exclaim, in an attempt to strike up a conversation.

They don't even flinch, sitting in the alert position, ready to strike something out of the ordinary.

Some thing's not right he thought to himself, a weapons demonstration doesn't usually involve such a level of secrecy and the obvious extra caution these men are taking, "We are in the most fucked up region in the Subcontinent" he thought, three nuclear powers fighting over a piece of land, that had become too much of an issue for anyone to give up on. We were on the safe side, he reminded himself, over and over again, as the Soldiers showed no signs of relenting, eventually, after several hours of gruelling travel in the back of a truck, he arrived at a place that he could not fathom. After carefully checking him the sentry allowed him entry in the compound, which didn't look any bit like an advanced facility. Several tin structures dotted the ground inside the camp. Some soldiers looking weary inside their LMG bunkers, Some others eating robotically in the dim light, without exchanging a word.

"This is it?"

"This is the Army demonstration Camp?"

"Yes" came a voice from his left,

"Captain Thevar, I am assigned to you here"

"Hello, Sir, I am Ar…."

"Arjun Joshi, Accurate Technologies, Yes, I know."

"Great Sir, May I just say it's really a plea.."

"Is this all the gear that you have?"

"Yes Sir"

"Good, please follow me, the jawans will take care of it."
"Right"

An Officer and a gentleman, they say, clearly he didn't attend the class for manners or common courtesy, he thought.

The Captain's manners are no longer my concern, I get ready to do the thing I have come here to do, I am greeted again by another sentry, who stands guard by a shed.
"Your thing's Sir"
"It's with another guy, he was just behind me"
"Thank you" he says and jets off behind me,

This place is getting uncanny, I am not sure if I am in the right place.

The sentry leaves me standing, while the Captain, who hadn't bothered to stop, had moved up quite a bit. I rushed up a little to meet him; He stops abruptly in front of a tin house,
"Your Quarters"
I stare blankly at him, what did he just say?
"I beg your pardon?"
"Yes"
"I didn't understand."
"Which part?"
"My quarters?"
"What didn't you understand about that?" he said, staring coldly.
"I wasn't aware I would be required to stay here"
"My instructions are to escort to your quarters, where you will stay"
"There has to be some sort of mistake, I wasn't aware that..."
"Mr Joshi, I am not concerned with anything; I have done all that I have been ordered to do. You have to spend the night here."
"Yes, but I have to inform the Hotel and the Driver"
"Not my concern."
He didn't even stand to acknowledge that the conversation was over, Asshole.

The Jawan came in with my bags and placed them inside the makeshift room. He pointed to the Jug of water and the Bed, and left without a word.

"What have I ever done to deserve this nonsense?"

The Light never went off inside the room; He spent the next 4 hours, trying to refresh the presentation. He went over the figures again and again, every technical aspect, every operational detail. At some point, he nodded off, only to awake on his bed a few hours later, still clutching a paper tightly. He looked around for his pack of cigarettes, found the lighter and came out. He didn't realise how cold it would be, shaking with the Cold, he lit his cigarette after trying three times and drew long puffs. He couldn't help but notice the diamonds in the sky above, never had he seen it so clear, or as many stars in the sky. The Milky way, he didn't even know what it looked like. It seemed almost magical.

The cigarette burned quickly in the wind, and after almost three puffs, he had reached the bud. He looked around for a toilet and remembered the sign from when he came in. Few minutes later, he came out relived and almost sleepy. No sooner had he opened his door, some chatter buried in the wind, caught his attention. "Guards no doubt", he thought to himself, maybe they have some noodles they can share, and he walked across the camp and made straight for the gate. Walking alone with the wind blowing, no village or city in the next 100 Km's, no real contact with the outside world, the camp as dead as a cemetery and it's also pitch dark, "Yup, Great Idea" he thought as he began contemplating, if he should have left his lodging at all. As soon as he came within 10 steps of the Gate, it became apparent the guards are not talking to each other. Both of them angled away from each other looking into the void. The voices continued,
"How can they not hear the voices? Or am I going crazy?"
A turn of the head, made him realise the voices are coming from the left, another tin room, he stared at it and realised that sounds were coming from there. A sudden flash of red light shone for a second along with what sounded like a buzzer. He was hooked, something was not right. Why would something like this happen out here in the middle of nowhere? Tracing his steps out carefully, he made it to one

of the windows of the structure, the window had been smoked out, so nothing was really visible, he hunched around to the door, which was slightly open. He opened it up slightly and peered inside to find it empty; he opened it completely and went inside.

I definitely heard voices in here! He thought. An empty room? What was this place? Maybe I am wrong about the voices but I saw the light for sure!

Dumbfounded he looked around and slowly moved out of the room. Best not to push my luck too far he mumbled. He came out and started slowly walking back to his room. He thought a little bit about the whole episode, but soon became overcome by sleep. Wasn't long before the snoring stared and everything else faded away.

He awoke to a Jawan, gripping his arm
"Wake up Sir"
"Huh?"
"Wake up please, please be ready for the presentation in 20 Minutes"
"What? I am not sure what you are talking about"
"20 Minutes, You have been informed!

He woke up as soon as the Jawan left the room. You have been informed, what are you? My mother?

He quickly dressed up, grabbed his notes and opened the door, 3 Jawans were waiting for him

"Follow us please"
"Sure, No Problem'"

The two took up position on both sides of him and one behind him,

"Captain Thevar?"
He did notice there was no sign of him, the vehicles seemed to be there, so he hadn't gone anywhere, the canteen tent seemed to almost full, but the rude Captain was not among them.

"We are going to him"

They walked him to the tin room, he had tried to explore the night before. They opened the door, the room was empty, the same way it was the previous night, They asked him to wait and marched outside.

"No Chairs, no furniture, no Computer? How am I going to do this presentation?"

"Mr Joshi"

He saw up, startled to hear a voice in the room.

I was right! There are voices here!

"Mr Joshi, If you wouldn't mind walking over to the window with both your Arms stretched out to your sides"

He followed. The Jawans ran a quick scan with metal detectors and some other instrument he didn't quite understand.

"All Clear!"

Now please go over to the switchboard that you see attached to the wall?"

He did as he was told

"Remove it please"

The Box had a small hole on the other side, and a slot for a card. "Insert your validation card and the key into it and return it to its position"

The room filled with a low hum, that like a small motor, a light flashed, similar to the one he had seen the night before. The ground moved and whole floor started descending into the ground.

"Holy Fuck! What is happening?"

"Mr Joshi, Welcome to Project Trident"

9

The mountains of Maharashtra come alive in the rains; the mighty Sahyadhis have much to offer not only the casual but also the avid wanderer. As was planned, I took up the mantle of calling everybody and getting everything in the right order, where to pick up whom and in what order, one thing, that changed was the obvious pecking order, the couples now wanted to be power couples, how would anyone leave us behind for last? No sir, That simply will not do, Also the most coveted seat, the one next to the drivers, was traditionally occupied by me but since the girls were coming, the seat would go to the better half of whoever drove the car, or whose car it may have been, usually I dislike sitting in the rows behind, My tall and somewhat bulky frame is best seated by the front row, I hate the airlines, where they simply charge a premium on the seats 1A and the ones near the wings, someone give those boys a Cookie. In any case, it didn't matter today, Riya was with me, I would have ridden on the top, as long as it meant spending time with her. The idea was to bring in Josh and Serena, Jigar and Shruti and Mayank and Sabina, opting out of the car, so they could have some more quality time together. That left me and the other two couples with a car that could seat the 6 of us quite comfortably. The large SUV's are always the favourites. I called up Riya and asked her to message me her address so I could come pick her up. The reply was prompt and within minutes, I was waiting near here home, with the rest of the Gang, since Mayank and his Girlfriend left early, she was busy taking some weird shots of the both of them and sending it to the other girls, what she was trying to prove was a mystery but only to me, not to the other girls, who had the entire cryptic message completely figured out. They talked about it in the Car,

I decided to step out and wait for Riya outside the Car, seemed only courteous. I saw them, those beautiful Kohl eyes, how can you forget them? She stepped out looking like a million bucks, I might as well have my entire Jaw to the ground, drool and everything, watching her make those 20 odd steps from the gateway to the car, seemed heavenly. I only hope she didn't see through me, I put on a small smile and waved to her. She got in; smiled, greeted everyone warmly and off we went. I was in the middle row, with a lot of space, a good comfortable distance away from her. Her perfume was on my mind, ever since she got down from her place and I am still trying not to stare at her, all this made me very, very uncomfortable. Thankfully with time, things subsided and a little and I got a bit comfortable with her presence around me.

The drive as always was lovely, except being held up before getting out of Mumbai. The traffic here is nothing short of appalling every single time. The minute we got out of its clutches and headed for the Hills, the frustrations became less apparent and eventually transformed into a calm reservoir of silence. I should have known she would break it.

"So you do this every weekend huh?"

"Yes"

"Always?"

"Mostly"

I'm not often chatty on trips; I tend to become a silent admirer of the roads and try to appreciate the subtle beauty in life. The sight of a family on a bike or the simple view from the window of a car. I talk, but mostly that's not what's really going on in my head. Usually no one, me included, knows what's going on in my head.

Today we head to Lonavala. An old favourite. I say old since it's no longer a staple of my trips. I usually tend to avoid it in favour of more beautiful and unspoiled locations. The entrance to the small hill town is laced with cars creating a bottleneck to the entrance of the main road, just off the express highway.. The mad cacophony of the horns and the efforts of ambitious bikers who try to inch out the smallest of gaps to pass through are anything but soothing. The main road has become Mumbai in rush hour. Somehow after an hour of standing in almost still traffic we get through to the main attraction. The reason Lonavala became famous in the first place. The high points of Tiger and Shivling. The points are now anything but scenic; they were perhaps 5 years ago. The place crawls with cars and people who are doing anything but looking out from the points. The people come in new cars and old, big and small, sometimes stuffed into buses and sometimes on foot. I hate the very sight off people doing touristy things; then again, I am a tourist. This is not my home.

I step off and hold the door open for her, she smiles at me when she leaves the car and walks towards the edge of the cliff, the same cliff, where I almost threw myself off a couple of years ago. No, not in attempted suicide, without the gory details, I did what happens to people when they become too drunk to differentiate up from down and reason from pure and utter stupidity. Fortunately, I had the good sense to avoid the edge on that night. Might have been for a very bad suicide story.

It's almost raining now, the slight drizzle alarms a few people who rush back to their cars. It doesn't even slightly deter Riya, she simply keeps walking and sits down on one of the rocks without saying a word to any other. I look for my friends who have conveniently scattered in different directions, with their better halves. I walk up to her and look at her for a few seconds as she stares off into the valley. She is calm, relaxed and at peace. It's almost unreal. I come around her and into her field of view. Our eyes meet and instead of saying anything, I simply smile and sit down on another rock not far from her and join her in admiring the view.

"Bravo!" comes the word

I look back, slightly surprised.

"First time you didn't say something."

"Well, it didn't need to be said"

"Right, you didn't ruin the moment by saying something; you just let the moment be. You were in it, rather than talking about it."

I simply smile and look back into the view.

"What do you think about when you look at something like that? "

"Is there something strange at looking at wide open pieces of Land that inspire City folk, or are we just zapped by the open space? I mean, is this what we desire? Wide open spaces? If so, why do we consent to being canned like fish and shuttled around in Metal boxes so we can do things that we don't like, to make money that we would spend on things that really don't interest us anyway?"

"You want life truths? How about the cold and simple fact, that we are trapped. Living a live that we don't want and for the most part we didn't determine. Our lives are determined by a standard which is set by other people. In fact, the biggest joke is that we do absolutely nothing for ourselves. The big house, the fancy car or the money is mostly just for other people." I say it with a smile, to hide my contempt for how society works.

"Chill dude. Look at this place, look at the view, Look at me"

I chuckle a little, not to seem a little embarrassed. I wasn't thinking of her the whole time, although now that she mentions it, it's not such a bad idea. So we steal some stares every now and then. I stand up after some time, and seat myself next to her.

"My, my, you are a little slow, but at least you get it."

"Slow? Get it? What?"

She lets out a generous laugh.
"Nothing." She says, still laughing, tucks her hair behind her ears, and

then takes my hand into hers, slightly pats it, looks at me and then back to the valley.
Wow!

10

Well, Things are moving in unexpected directions. He thought to himself, his usual idea of making presentations did not involve subterranean locations or the kind of up tightness that goes along with being an unwelcome outsider to people with automatic weapons who seemingly have itchy trigger fingers, the lift, such as it is stops after a good 15 minutes and ends a very uncomfortable silence.

"Good Morning Mr Joshi."

"Morning Captain, You surely got the Jump on me." he tries a little humour.

"Yes, I am sure we all did, now if you would follow me" He replies coldly again

Captain Thevar should be called Captain Stone. Wasn't he ever hugged as a child? He thought as he regretted using that approach with him. He decided to keep quiet the remainder of the way.

The door simply read, "Project Head" with a Trident whose tips seemed to be made of lightning was positioned upright.

Project Trident, this is what the man talked about.

Captain Thevar walked inside after 2 loud knocks at the door asked for permission to get me in and marched outside with the dismissal of the Officer sitting behind the Desk. He didn't look at him, simply kept looking down and kept on marking positions on a map.

"Are you going to stand there or have a seat?"

"Was just waiting for permission, Sir"

"You didn't make your presence felt. I had to look up to find you. It's a strain in people I find... undesirable"

"Oh, well, sorry Sir."

"My name is Arjun Joshi from..."

"Accurate Technologies, can we please move beyond the obvious? I know who you are and why you are here, please don't test my patience, I assure you it's not very flexible"

Seems this guy's charming personality has rubbed off everyone in the base. At least now I know where they all get their winning charm from.

I had read the report on Colonel Brar. It described him as easily irritable, highly patriotic, and a bit of an eccentric when it came to running his troops. He was highly decorated during the Kargil War having secured 2 bunkers while fighting with a bullet lodged in his right leg, and shrapnel wound to his stomach. He personally saved more than 6 men during the war and was a legend among the Troops who have served under him. His ideas on how to bolster the security of the borders fell on deaf ears after the wars; instead he was promoted and put in charge of the acquisitions office of the Army, where each step he would take would have to be vetted by the higher ups. It was a manoeuvre to keep him in check, his hostile attitude to the enemy was almost at the edge of inciting another war. He has been quite the pencil pusher ever since. Trying to modernise it in any way possible.

"Your predecessor had kept us in the dark for quite some time, I hope you can deliver."

"I hope so too Sir May I begin?"

"No let me, before you go off on your quite unnecessary babble on your supposed new technology, I would like to tell you, there is no need for it. The only reason you are sitting on the table across from me is because I need a Demonstration, not a Presentation. If you have anything to the contrary, I suggest you leave now."

"A demonstration? Sir, I wasn't aware I was supposed to demonstrate, I was here to talk about the systems and get your opinion on the new builds we have done"

"I have changed my mind, I need to see it in action, not wait 10 years for it."

"That would be quite difficult, as I don't have any of the equipment with me Sir."

"It arrived last night and is currently held as us, your superiors have been informed, and they also assured me that you could do it."

Information pieced together in his head, the light from last night, no contact from his Boss, the secrecy regarding the place.

"So can you do it, or have you simply wasted my time by coming here?"
It's one of the rare times that your boss comes into your mind, along with all you could gain or all you could lose, the brilliance of it, the horror of it. Your mouth opens all by itself.

"Yes, I can give you a demonstration, although, I would have to get some codes from my office first"

"You may" he said, pointing to the phone on his desk.

"May I have some conversation in private?"

"I am afraid that won't be possible, as all communication in and out of the base is monitored and .regulated. There is no such thing as a private conversation out of this facility."

"Very well" He picked up the phone and called the number

"Sir, this is Joshi"

"Heaven's Sake Joshi, you have any concept of keeping in touch? Do you not know how tight this ship is supposed to be running right now?"

"Yes Sir, I do Sir, I am sitting across from Colonel Brar right now"

His voice dropped,

"Joshi, where are you?"

"I am not quite sure about that Sir, but that's not why I have called. Well, you see Sir, they are asking for a Demo."

"Yes, I know, they asked for the Tech, I had them flown out on priority."

"Sir?"

"Come on, don't be such a baby. You know the company needs you to do this right now; it's about the company Arjun, our Colleagues, and our Investors, who have put so much faith in us. Arjun, we are like a family aren't we?"

From Joshi to Arjun. That was quick, he thought as he still pondered over the gravity of the situation he was in.

"When you love your family, your family loves you back. I know you can do it Arjun, we trust you over here."

"Do it for the company.", "Family" could he get any more plain in hiding his sheer terror of what was happening? The man talked over the phone, while the Colonel looked as if, his patience was wearing off. He had only had 2 tries before and both times, he almost blew it. He was a Salesman, not an Operator.

"Ok Sir, will do it, Although Let me remind you that the ACE (Advanced Combat Enhancer) still has the..."

"Yes yes Joshi, I am aware of that. Best of Luck"

Bastard. He thought as he readied himself for the biggest hour of his professional life.

"Should we move Sir?"

"Yes." He rings a buzzer and a soldier comes in, he opens a small cabinet and gives a card to the Colonel, he keeps it in his pocket as they exit the room.

The skeletal staff of the installation is baffling, for someone who keeps some of the top end stuff, they sure seem to have very low security.

They turn to go to the elevator and the boxes are already loaded in Advance.

"We   are   going   back   up,   Sir?"

"Well, I can't have a demo down here, can I?" His voice is condescending; perhaps I walked into that one.

After 15 minutes of the slow ride to the Surface, My eyes are blinded by the sunlight as I step outside in the dusty compound. Some more Containers are brought to the surface and it's time to begin.

"Sir, if you could insert your card in the panel and put in your assigned pin?" The Colonel does what he is told and I follow the procedure.   Once the field authorization is done, the base immediately receives a call from Accurate Technologies, trying to verify if we tried to open the Containers, after confirming the Identities of Myself and Colonel Brar. The man hands up the phone and asks us to wait 2 minutes.

I look at the Colonel as he waits; he simply looks at his base, not a hint of anticipation in him. He is collected and probably not even interested in what we have to offer, or maybe he has seen this Tech a hundred times before, we are not the only high tech weapons manufacturer in India.

The Containers beep. The company has verified the three tier security system and disabled the trigger mechanism for a small explosive charge. Just in case someone tried to open it the wrong way or a way to destroy the contents if the company didn't want it to be seen.

We could hear the internal locks snapping and the lids of the containers popping up ever so slightly and then in a swift motion, the front sides swung open while the Top door seemed locked in its position.

He wanted to frown right there, There goes the first impression he thought. Collecting his wits, he drew in a breath of air and some with some conjured confidence, he walked up to the first container, opened up the Top Door, revealing the contents inside and said loudly

"Colonel, It is my pleasure to introduce you, to the ACE "

The Colonel looked inside, and smiled.

11

We didn't say anything much to each other for the rest of the trip; our eyes did most of the talking. The trip back was mostly uneventful with embarrassing, often detailed tales being retold for the umpteenth time for the simple pleasure that is derived from berating your fellow mates. Other than the odd laugh and mostly forced smiles, I don't do very much. She doesn't seem bothered much and keeps up her jovial demeanour. After all, she did have a very good day, I am more than sure of it.

I drop her below her Apartment, true to my word, before 10 and give a quick call home, telling them how much of an impossibility it is for me to return home, since I had been deeply implored to spend the night at one of our friends Villa, since it's a Saturday and they usually detest the night driving option, they yield, with a condition of making it back early the next day. The exercise of course is done so I can check in on Arun and spend the night at his place, telling him of my adventure and probably take his mind of the current series of unfortunate events he seems to be going through. I am quite sure, listening to a friend doing well, might just be the catalyst he needs to get himself off the couch and back into the fighting man I once knew and to a some degree looked up to. He wasn't in such good shape, when I last left him. I make a quick call to confirm his availability for the evening and also to make sure that he has the extra bed. I head first to the Wine shop to pick up the essentials and some Snacks and cigarettes on the way; this should make for an interesting night.

I wait for the elevator with a middle aged lady who looks at my bags and instantly brands me either a Gangster, Sexual deviant or perhaps worse. You can easily tell from the long drawn out stares and the slight frown that remains plastered to her face. That she is secretly wishing I would have been better off locked in some jail somewhere. The Lift arrives and I can see how much this Lady detests being in the same space as me. The awful lifts at Arun's building have been in need of dire repair for the last 10 years. Someone only attends to the damned thing once it breaks down so the ride up to the 14th floor is especially slow and frustrating to the Lady. I sometimes have fun with them, whistling randomly or playing odd songs on my phone. Most of it is meant in harmless fun, since she seemed in so much of a hurry to judge me just because I have Beer in my hands. I ask her if she knows Arun, she nods and displays further signs she is not interested in talking to me. Ahh, wonderful Judgemental people always make for great travel companions

I ring the bell and Arun opens it after asking who is at the door. He opens it, visibly silent and possibly a little embarrassed since our last encounter. I make quick reassurances that all is fine and he needn't worry about anything.

"So,, back again for a talk?"

"No buddy, just a hit of Alcohol"

"Hmm, What have you got for me?"

"Cool beer and a promise of a buzz, by the way, I might have scared the lady a floor down with all the booze, she might have boarded up her house in anticipation that I or possibly we might do something"

Don't worry about her, all she can do is gossip about me. Call her children close like a Mother Hen when the Eagle comes swooping by.

We sit down and light up a cigarette, popping open the bottles of beer and silently slipping into a good time.

How was Riya today? Any luck with her?

Plenty, I think we connected today, I can definitely imagine more time with her in the future.

You know your parents will be pissed when they find out about the big affair.

We shall cross that bridge when we get there my friend.

A small chuckle follows my imagining of the day I would tell my Parents, if I would ever take this girl home.

The beer flows easy and soon, both of us have a good buzz going. My phone rings and its Riya,

"Asleep?"

"For you, never."

"Please..."

I smirk slightly; the beer isn't helping me put a restraint on my mouth, all my cheesiness might just be revealed.

"No, tell me, what's up?"

"Had an awesome day, thanks so much for it. Thank your friends for me too."

"Will do."

Arun butts in, teasing me. Riya listens to the talk and laughs, she gets it.

"Are you drunk?"

"Well, only slightly, although I can pretty much say my friend would be heading to the nearest bathroom any time."

"Well, not having been drunk too often myself, Could I ask something to you?

"Of course anything,"

"Do people usually tend to tell the truth when being drunk?"

"Sure, depends on how drunk you are?"

"How much are you?"

"I   am   four   bottles   true."

"Then tell me, how would you like to join me on a big tour?"

"Tour, where?"

"I have been dreaming to go to Ladakh for some time."

"Ummm... ok, how many people coming along for the trip?" I asked, just to make sure, she didn't mean just us.

"Around 4, who have confirmed until now"

"We were planning to leave and I thought, maybe you would like it"

"Like it?"

"Yes, I mean, you did say that you loved travelling a lot and seeing new places"

There is a momentary pause in her voice, a slight shift from her usually controlled voice to that of one momentarily shaky and perhaps even a tinge of hopefulness. I let it hang for just a few seconds

"Hello?"

"Yes, I am right here." I reassure her. The game has changed, until now; I was the one waiting for the answers, now this girl is waiting for me too. How silly are the games we play in Love.

"Oh, I though the call had dropped."

"Ok." I can't help but smile a little. I think I will extend this a little more. She deserves to be left in middle just a little bit more; after all she has put me through.

"Well, what do you think?"

"I really don't know, when are you guys leaving?"

"This week, most probably"

"What???"

"Yeah, I know its short notice but we just sort of decided. I have a lot of leaves saved up and the pilots strike just stopped"

"Ummm." She sure knows how to kill a buzz. Wow, this girl defines the meaning of spontaneous. What do I do now?

"Truth be told, I wanted to leave this winter but the weather conditions now are perfect"

"What? Perfect? I just read today that the region is experiencing some freak weather"

"Exactly. We wanted to do a snow leopard spotting. They only come down from their heights when you have really cold weather. A friend of mine thinks it's a great idea to go now and beat the crowds as well the prices."

"This friend of yours is a wildlife expert, is he?"

"No just common sense, he says"

"Common sense? And you are willing to put your life in danger on the word of this friend?"

"I know it sounds a little farfetched but I think it has some logic in it"

I don't know how to answer now, the prospect does seem promising and the girl probably wants to close the deal, otherwise she wouldn't have invited me on this trip anyway. Oh why does my life have to be covered in dilemma?

"OK. Done"

"Done? Like that?"

"Just like that"

At this juncture, she probably thinks that I am too gullible and would have agreed to anything. She isn't wrong. I would have agreed to anything. So what if I don't have leaves or what if I am almost out of money. I make a smug face, when I catch Arun from the corner of my eye. I am almost tempted to ask. Should I?

"Hey, one more thing, can a friend of mine join in? I think he needs a break and this would be the perfect opportunity"

Arun is looking a little uneasy and maybe his buzz is about to die but he doesn't pay much attention to my talks, he knows its Riya on the other line. He has been surprisingly quiet.

"A friend? Hmm I guess so."

"Cool, send me the flight details and we shall get on it right away."

"Thanks for being a sport and coming on such short notice"

"Ohh yeah... Don't mention it"

I look at Arun now, a moment of silence passes between us..

"You are making your evil face again aren't you?"

I burst out laughing, the man is blind but somehow he always sees through me

"Oh yes, my friend. You are going to like it"

"I already know that I am not going to like what you say. This is something bad."

"Guess what!"

"Oh fuck off, I don't want to"

"You me and Riya are going to Ladakh!"

"Hold on there.. I don't remember saying yes!"

"I don't remember asking you!" I retort playfully, this is a lost battle, he isn't going to win this one.

"I don't have leaves or anything.. I will have to take Unplanned."

"So what? You make plenty of money! Won't matter if you don't make some for a few days"

"But..."

"Shut up! I already know, you are dying to come. Now stop acting like this isn't what you want too"

He chuckles,

"Oh, you also need to float me some money for the trip, with me being broke and all"

"You're an asshole!"

He lets out a smile which just confirms all that I have just said and we toast one more time to the mountains and continue to drown ourselves in more Alcohol.

11

All high durability actuators.
Titanium-Magnesium Alloy outer hull.
High grade Carbon fibre and kevlar interior weaving.
Deployable high stress capable spring action mobility enhancers tied in with the actuators.
Deployable fire shield
Deployable High Voltage disruptors
Deployable short range mini Missiles
Standard issue 9mm high speed automatic machine guns on both arms. Both holding 500 rounds meach.
Optional TX-941 assault rifle, 25 caliber rounds
Weighing only 40 kilos without TX-941
Augmented strength and durability during Combat situations.
Optional B1 assault rifle, 25 caliber rounds

While I give him the sales pitch, The Colonel circles around the ACE, getting close every now and then to examine some parts. He is smiling now, although slightly. He obviously doesn't want to give away his excitement to a salesman because that's what I essentially am, a glorified salesman.

"25 Caliber? That's a strange number for a rifle."

"We realise that sir, We wanted to give you more penetration power than the regular assault rifles but not the heavy lifting problems of the. 50 Caliber System"

"Plus, only you would supply the Ammunition, would I be correct in assuming that?" he asks a little condescendingly.

"Yes Sir, No one could make it better" I reply firmly

"Sure sure" probably figuring out that we designed it so, no one else could manufacture it.

"May I also point out the ACE is designed as a single as well as multiple attack solution.
A single soldier in the ACE system is more destructive than at least a 10man patrol team. Get a 10 man ACE team and you have the capacity to hold a position against a large force or attack an asset with minimum or no casualties. Each system is unique in the sense that it is completely customizable to the fighting style of the Unit and the particular soldier. You want a Demolitions expert in the team, take away the 9mm unit and install a high-explosive unit. So you want a climber? The entire system can refitted to accommodate a climbing set-up and weapons can be put on non-priority. The modules can be changed, added and removed to your specific need at a specific time. It is the complete system. This is the future of warfare."

This time I hold his complete attention, he is, without a doubt really interested, he probably wasn't expecting it to be so good. He looks at the ACE intensely, almost hypnotised by it. The possibilities seem mind boggling to him.

"You can use just the mobility unit, or just the fire power unit or just the heavy protection unit. It's all up to you."

"Does it work? Or is it just a model?"

"Of course it does Sir, If I could have one of you men to demonstrate"

"No"

"Sir?"

"I said no. Show it to me with you in it" He says calmly without even thinking about it.

"Oh but Sir, I am not rated to handle it"

"Your company's selling point was that a buffoon with no training can handle it" I cringe hearing that, having had enough of his condescension. I frown, which I don't hide. He sees it, a little conscious of what he has said.

Without a second thought, he picks up a small control switch from the container and presses a button, a small button; the suit opens and is ready to receive an operator. Having being trained only enough to perhaps accommodate this eventuality, he reluctantly moves in closer, with each step his heart rate increases, his palms are now sweaty and he tries to resist the slight shiver that crawls though his body.

The suit is cold and feels like an immovable rock, he gets in and restrains himself, every detail observed diligently by the Colonel and his men, whose attention now seems to be piqued. With the familiar sound of motors whirring, the contraption comes to life and the lower arches rise to lift him a full metre over the ground. He wears the helmet and the HUD (heads up display) lights up to show the basic information including his GPS, battery strength and operational mode, its set to demo. For the first time in many days, almost feeling giddy with power, he faces the Soldiers, who look noticeably awestruck and a little intimidated.

Without looking at the Colonel, Captain Thevar walks up to the ACE, observing this titan,

Arjun's helmet opens and he holds out this arm and shows it off to the Officer with a large smile.

"So, what do you think.....?"

Before he can finish his question, warm blood splatters over his face and his mouth opens with disbelief and horror to what he sees in front of him

12

The Flight tickets were more expensive than what I would have sold my kidneys for, Damn! This love business is not for the faint of heart, or for those who are miserly. Luckily Arun paid for the tickets this time and told me to give him the money whenever I could. How could a girl really ever dislike him? Oh yes, there was a slight issue with the fact that he wasn't able to see. I catch up on some news on my phone and some messages for my overbearing mother who was not completely on board with this Ladakh plan because it meant taking leaves from the Office. People all around the airport usually keep to themselves and have a marked air of superiority. Everyone looks or at least tries to look like someone important and most have got this opportunity by searching for the lowest possible air ticket and are in fact true misers themselves. I bring up the topic with Arun, who seems mildly nervous and keeps asking to visit the Smoking zone.

I spot Riya form a distance, everything else fades, Tunnel Vision, That's what they call it, isn't it When everything else fails and all you see the light at the end of the tunnel. Damn my cheesy brain. She takes quite some time to analyse Arun, not sure what all that was about. Behind her was a friend of hers, quite frankly one that I wasn't keen on meeting.

He nods and says "Hi", almost ignoring me and Arun entirely, which instantly suggests that he isn't happy to see us. He walks with a gum in his mouth and wears Sunglasses inside the airport and his earphones are still attached firmly to his ears but what irritates me the most is his hat. Why that fad caught on at all is still a mystery. He walks up to the security check in guard; his body language speaks of nothing but contempt. Needless to say, I take an instant dislike to him. Arun does too and he can't even see the guy. He asks me to describe him and frowns even more. "Constipated prick" he mumbles softly, only loud enough for me and him to hear. Riya catches us giggling like little girls and comes over.

"So what are you gossiping about?"

"Your friend there."

.

"What about him?"

I roll my eyes and show the same contempt he showed me some moments ago.

"Hey, be nice, he is one of my oldest friends."

"Let me guess, He wasn't happy when you told him I was about to come along too."

"Well..."

"Forget it; I am sorry I brought it up. As long as we are here, doesn't matter"

"You are a sweetheart!"

"Rohan's story is a little complicated, He was my friend right through college and..."

"Then he proposed and you said no."

"Are you psychic?"

"No but you are a pretty girl and I can do the Math"

We laugh together looking into each other's eyes. I can feel the bond growing strong with her, every moment its growing deeper and deeper. I feel for Rohan, just a little bit, I was where he is several years ago and frankly it's not a very nice place to be but, in any case, he isn't getting my girl. Riya goes away for a bit and Rohan comes and sits down right next to me, without uttering a single word.

The deafening silence is too much to take and I open up my Bag to check my camera and clear out some pictures from the last time. He has a look at my camera and for the first time, in a non-condescending tone, asks me,

"Is that, like a Removable lens cameras"

"Yes, it's a DSLR."

"Cool, Cool, My uncle has one" he says still rolling over that gum in his mouth and still speaking with a bit of an accent.

"They are like really cheap now right? Only for a lakh or something"

"The lower end ones are around 20,000 so yeah, they are a little cheap." I say, trying to sound as friendly as possible. The Earlier statement still rings in my head. Really cheap, like a Lakh?

"Yeah Dude, I was like, thinking of getting one, People say the clarity is like, Amazing"

"True."

"So, What do you do man?"

"Oh, I am Photographer."

"Cool Cool, So, you do events and stuff?"

"Yes, marriages, pre wedding and architecture shoots primarily I am working under another photographer right now."

"So you have studied it or something?"

"Uh. No, I always had a passion for photography and eventually shifted careers."

"So, you have studied something else."

"Yeah, Commerce."

Why is he chatty all of a sudden? His accent is strange and what's stranger is he has his hat on and on the hat he has pulled up his hoodie. Was this the guy who suggested seeing snow leopards? How was this even possible? This Buffoon? It's quite possible that this man here, is sizing me up and that "Really cheap" comment was most probably meant to show me how rich he was. Not to take away any thunder from the women but men do the sizing up and job pretty well too. While some women look at purses, dresses and make up. Men try comparing the size of their wallets, their social status and their bodies, usually in that order. Some may change if they are well endowed physically. Fortunately he hasn't begun flexing his muscles at me, although he does look like he goes to the Gym.

Riya seats herself between me and him and tells him that Shilpa is all ready and waiting to board from Delhi. Shilpa is another College friend of Riya, both were in the same college and then she moved to Delhi for a Job. They are essentially one group from College days. I wanted to go alone with Riya but now this has turned in to a college reunion with me and Arun being unwitting guests. Still, it must have taken her a lot of convincing to allow me and Arun to tag along I think about that when the Boarding call for the plane is announced and we proceed toward the boarding gate. Arun and me go in together and find our seats and settle down. Arun wants to sit in the window seat. I try to explain the pointlessness of that request but he won't budge. Why some people, behave like they do, is something that I don't think I will be privy to for a long time. It just escapes me, so now I sit in the middle and the Aisle seat, I am hopeful will be occupied by Riya. She walks in behind us, contemplates sitting next to me and changes her mind when she sees Rohan sitting Alone. The seat is subsequently occupied by a rather large and loud gentleman, who makes sure his voice is heard throughout the plane, even when he talking through his phone. I look back and see Riya laughing at my dilemma with her hand covering her mouth. Rohan sits motionless, noticeably disgruntled. The plane is sealed and after the customary safety briefing by the bored to death Air hostess who are probably trying their best to hide their feelings of "How many times must I do this before I die?" with a pleasant smile.

The plane taxis on to the runway and my heart starts beating a little faster. I wouldn't say I have a fear of flying but every time the plane takes off, I am always a little nervous. The plane rises up, banks a little too sharply to the left and we are off our way to Delhi. The Seat belt signs are off and we relax for the trip to Delhi.

13

Arjun's face was bloody and Captain Thevar lay on the ground with a hole in his head. He is still in shock, eyes wide open, breathing heavily and scared stiff. The Soldiers are now alert and Colonel Brar face is beyond description. As the pool of blood around Captain Thevar's head grows, the soldiers have started remembering their training and are now raising their guns towards Arjun. The Colonel's Scream startle him as he sees the lifeless body the body.

"What have you done????? What have you done??????"

"No! No! I haven't done anything!" He says being defensive.

"I saw you raise your guns, you murdered him!!"

"No, No, I haven't fired"

"Jawans! Take him into custody" Colonel Brar screams

Instinctively, he moves and raises his hands in front of him gesturing that he didn't do it , not realising he is still inside the suit. The Jawans have raised their guns at him but are probably intimidated by the suit. All of them stand for a moment's pause, everyone has frozen. One of Jawans right behind the body of Captain Thevar musters some courage and starts walking towards Arjun, emboldened by this move the others, now start closing in on him. Realising the best way to deal with this now is to give in to their custody; Arjun suddenly tries to raise his Arms over his head, signalling surrender. His sudden movement spooks the Jawans closing in on him and one of them opens fire and the rest of them fire without hesitation. In the barrage of fire and bullets ricocheting off the suit, Arjun panics and starts moving his hands around. The barrage is enormous till another

Soldier drops dead on the ground right next to Captain Thevar. The others are horrified at the sight and the firing stops. They pummelled the suit with so many bullets and yet, there he stands as if nothing happened and now another man lies dead. Arjun looks just as shocked as before and looks at the soldiers saying

"I didn't do it! I didn't do it!"

Colonel Brar looks just as shocked as the others. This time, not because a soldier had died but he is shocked to see the amount of abuse the ACE can bear. They must have gotten off at least 200 rounds! How is he still standing? He orders his men to not fire and make their way back to safer distance. The Soldiers obey instantly, probably not wanting to stay in the same place that the machine was standing. Arjun Screams on the top of his Voice.

"Colonel, there's some mistake, something is wrong. I didn't fire! Please believe me!"

"Don't you dare move or I'll fire so many bullets that there won't be a body left to burn"

"Ok...Ok Just calm down, lets everybody calm down and let me figure out what's going on"

"Didn't you hear me the first time Motherfucker? Move and I will end you!"

Arjun is shaking with fear, Adrenaline is rushing through his entire body, he is sick to his stomach and feels as if he is about to pass out. The entire base heard the commotion and the loud firing that ensued and now every soldier on the Base has arrived with a Gun in his hands and the sights are all trained on Arjun.

The Colonel speaks firmly and with Authority,

"Raise your hands in the air slowly and turn around."

Arjun complies and does what he is asked.

"Now kneel and put your face on the ground"

Arjun starts crying examining his situation but does exactly what he is told.

The Colonel signals to a group of Soldiers to start moving towards the now immobile Arjun. They approach him cautiously while never letting him out of their Gun sights. As they make their way to him, they are still wondering how to get him out of the suit. They look at each other a little puzzled, never having encountered this kind of situation before. They reach Arjun but find that the Suits Arms are too large to be tied and that a rope simply wouldn't hold him. They start throwing suggestions around and wondering just a little bit as to how to constrain him

"Please! I didn't do anything!" Arjun pleads while crying.

"Shut Up! Stay Down!" the jawans order him.

"No Please, I will get out of the suit!" Arjun offers, He turns around much to the shock of the Soldiers who are beside him, he tries to remember the protocol to get himself out of the suit.

"Colonel!" he cries. "I am coming out of the suit! Don't Fire!"

"Stay down!" is the stern reply.

It's too late. Arjun is already up and trying to get out of suit.

Instantaneously, the Colonel Orders
"Fire!"

The barrage begins again, this time every soldier in the base is shooting and they are all shooting for blood, they see their fellow soldiers lying on the floor and are outraged by that sight. They fire blindly in short bursts and one even comes closer to try to bayonet

Arjun while he is inside the suit. Arjun moves around and in an instant, the adrenaline makes him do one of the two things the chemical is meant to do. With a swift elbow strike, he pushes the Jawan aside and runs as fast as he can. Anywhere but here, he thinks to himself. The suit is reading his vital signs and it reads the increased neural information going to his lower body and reacts by diverting energy to the lower actuators, increasing his speed tremendously. Within Seconds, the speed of the suit brings him beyond the effective range of the Soldiers and is rushing wildly into the open desert and Mountains. All this time, his mind is blank, all other processes have stopped, he thinks only of running and nothing else. The how and the why aren't important. Living is.

Highly camouflaged, and lying around a pile of rocks only 800 yards away, a face behind a rifle sees the suit in full sprint and the men who chase behind it. He remains motionless but smiles.

14

Kushok Bakula Rimpochee Airport, Leh.

It's been a long flight; Shilpa boarded from Delhi and was the girliest girl I had ever met. Pixie cut, matching pink shoes and Pink backpack with Loads of doodles on it and as I learnt to my dread. A compulsive selfie taker, the moment she boarded the plane, she took a selfie, she took one again when meeting with her old college buddies, and she then proceeded to take one more picture of just her and Riya. Riya quickly introduced me to her and I smiled and waved from my seat. Arun was still sleeping. While the flight took off again from Delhi to Leh. I could hear the trio going on nonstop till the time we landed in Leh. I switched my phone on, and lo and behold, she had even sent me a friend request. I went through her profile and yes, all the selfies had been promptly uploaded with non-imaginative captions for all of them, Including one from Rumi. What is it people and Rumi quotes? Half the people who upload Rumi updates have no idea who he even is! They would be stunned into silence if you even ask them if they knew any of his works, or even his full name, or even when he lived. Attention hungry idiots.

We deboard the plane and see the beautiful vistas which await us. The Leh airport is probably the Highest Airport in India, although I had heard of higher landings in Siachen, clearly this was the only airport accessible to Civilians. We walk towards the exit while Arun is offered a wheelchair when we get down from the plane.

"Are you blind?" Asks Arun when he hears the Wheelchair offer

The crew seem a little taken aback, their offer of generosity seems so sincere to them.

"I asked you if you were blind, I asked you that question because, if you weren't, you would have seen that all of my body parts function normally, except my eyes. Or is it commonplace around here to wheel blind people out of the airport as soon as you find about them?"

The crew still don't get it. I smile a little and quickly diffuse the situation by thanking them and reassuring them that a Wheelchair won't be required today.

"Every time! What idiots man" Snarls Arun privately

"You always have a fantastic reply to them"

As is the case with every airport in India and probably every Airport in the world, the Taximen outside scream and put on a spectacle to attract the tourists. Tourism has grown here in leaps and bounds and with tourism; the region has attracted some much needed money and development. Rohan asks us to stop and calls a number from his phone. Within minutes a sharply dressed man called Tashi shows up, warmly greets us and takes us to the hotel we had booked. Now came the problem, since originally there were only two rooms booked, one for the Girls and just one for Rohan. It now seemed as if, all the three boys would end up spending the night together. Apparently that didn't go well with Rohan as he promptly went up to the Hotel manager to request another room. By the Time we set our luggage and began settling in, Rohan came back with his head hung in disgust carrying the bad news, that the Hotel doesn't have any more rooms available currently as they are undergoing maintenance and getting ready for the tourist season which is just around the corner. There is one other room but since the person occupying that room hasn't come back yet, they are not sure what they will do with that room. Rohan was apparently convinced by the receptionist that in case the person did not show up for another day, they would empty the room and hand over that room off to him. So seems like he was stuck with us. He tried convincing the girls to move out into another Hotel but since they had already opened up their suitcases and were getting ready to freshen up and relax, so that was a lost cause. He came over, noticeably unhappy. I tried lightening up the mood a little by the odd jokes about how badly we both farted and he was going to have it tonight but Rohan smiled and said plainly that, it wasn't that he had any problems with us, it was just that he liked his privacy and always stayed in a single room wherever we went. A moment of awkward silence passed between us, with Arun finally speaking

"Well, don't worry about walking around naked with me around, Benefits of living with a blind man include that they just can't really see things that you don't want them to."

I let out a generous laugh and Rohan laughs too but only a little. He is clearly not as used to poking fun at Arun's Blindness as much as I am. Even though that sounds terrible. Rohan is finally comfortable with the fact that he must for better or worse share the room with us.

As the afternoon is over and evening descends, we ask him politely, if he wants to join us for a walk, He refuses citing the high altitude and how we must also resist the urge for the sake of our health. Arun is convinced instantly, or maybe it's just that he is being lethargic. I walk over to the girls rooms and knock on the door. "Come in" is the reply

"Hey! What's up?" it's only Shilpa sitting with two pillows on her lap

"Tired yaa!, didn't sleep also properly"

"Why what's wrong? And where is Riya?"

"She is taking a bath again, second one since we got here, intent on wasting every drop that the hotel has."

We both smile and I look out the window, it's snowing just a bit,

"Ooh, lets all go for a walk!"

"I actually came in to ask you guys the same question."

She rushes up to the bathroom door and asks Riya, if tells her if she wants to take a walk and that it's snowing slightly. When she says give me 2 minutes, she comes back and sits down on the bed again.

"So, I know all about you guys" she mentions with a sly smile.

I go from laid back to instantly attentive and alert, what does she know?

"Oh yeah? What's that?" I ask playfully

"Oh, I am not going to tell you so easily." she says all the time, smiling like a little girl.

Riya comes out from the Bathroom, looking like a vision. I am mesmerised by her and can't seem to take my eyes off, Shilpa snaps me out of it and asks me to if I want to go down and wait in the lobby while they came down. As the door shuts, both girls let out loud laughs and I am reminded how much I need to look away sometimes. The walk through the markets is great and gives me some time to bond with Riya and Shilpa and of course, Shilpa carries around a Selfie stick which she uses every 10 minutes to take a photo. Some of them are of me and Riya, maybe it's a good thing, she is doing the photo documentation for us. There are no romantic advances today, just a time for friends and laughter we have a nice evening and after dinner make our way back to the Hotel. I open up my room to find Arun and Rohan sleeping on the bed, i pull out the sofa and within minutes, I am asleep. Tomorrow will be exiting.

15

The thin air of high altitude, the dryness of this desert, all he gulped large mouthfuls of, as he ran and jumped across every hurdle in his path. The suit gleamed in the sun and made him visible to any eyes watching him. He had wanted to stop for a minutes now, sensing that danger was behind him and while his legs made lactic acid and burned with the ferocity of actual fire and his lungs felt as if they could blow, he wouldn't stop, he couldn't. He looked back, hoping to see a horde following him but there was no one, not a soul. Taken aback, he slowed down to a halt and seemed confused. While sweat poured out from his forehead to his eyebrows and to his eyes, his lungs welcomed the opportunity. He could finally contemplate the situation he was in. Back at the base, 2 soldiers lay dead and the entire episode happened because of me. Someone back at Design made a big, idiotic, disastrous mistake and now he was going to pay for it.

"Think!"
He said aloud, frustrated with his situation, it was only going to get worse from here, what he thought was ging to be a normal presentation was turning out to be the most eventful chapter of his life. He looked around frantically trying to find his bearings.

"Mountains, mountains everywhere! Where the hell am I?

Although he didn't realise it, Arun ran for over an hour, normally impossible for any human being not conditioned to this altitude but there was one major difference, he was in the ace. The suit was not merely an augmentation but also, a computer was bundled into the system with smart software that could mimic the human body's central nervous system, detect highs and lows in the dopamine levels, and most importantly, Adrenaline. As soon as Arun started running, the suit calculated that the operator is in grave danger with the levels spiked up the way they were, it redirected all of its energy to lower part of the system making him feel that it was him doing all the running but, in fact it was the suit. It took a minimal toll on the body but did what it needed to do.

Arun looked around his hands, the short scratches to the suit from where the bullets had ricocheted off. He felt more helpless than he ever did in life.

"Wait! The GPS" he said to himself.

"ACE! Start GPS"

In an instant the HUD (Heads up Display) lit up with words flashing on them.

...GPS unavailable- Unit not installed...

"What??? GPS unit not installed? How can that be?"

"OK, OK the distress beacon, that should alert the HQ of my location"

"ACE, Begin distress beacon"

... Radio not installed...

...Continue with Visual and Audio distress signal?...

"Yes"

...Commencing flare deployment and audio distress signal...

With the sound of a firecracker, a flare shot out from the back of the ACE and went straight up. The siren started ringing from the small loudspeakers installed. The flare shot up in the sky quickly disappeared into the light of the day as Arun saw disappointingly; the sound from the Sirens was making him cringe. He had few options left. He thought of tracing his steps back to the base but that would have been impossible, he had no idea of where he had come from and where he stood, he was in the shadow of a mountain and in front of him lied a valley covered with fresh snow. He stood around with the sirens going on full volume for half an hour till he could take the sound no more.

"ACE, Stop Distress signal"

His nerves had calmed down a bit and he was breathing a little easy now, he wondered where the soldiers must be and how they were tracking him down, surely a call to his HQ must have been relayed about his "demonstration" and despised the ACE team for making a gigantic error, the blood of two soldiers was on his hands and the people there wouldn't forget it. He thought of all this in the afternoon Sun and decided the only logical way to get out of this situation was to try and retrace his steps back to the base and face whatever came his way. He turned around to see the boulder he had passed and started walking towards it. As he started A Sharp noise resonated throughout the suit, the kind that a pebble makes when thrown at metal. A second later, a slight pop was heard from the direction he was facing. Confused by this, he stopped and squinted at the direction of the noise. In the next instant, he saw a small flash, followed by a clink that came from the suit and the pop that came from a distance. He instantly put two and two together, someone was shooting at him! He waved his hands around like a mad man, Screaming

"Don't Shoot! Don't Shoot! I Surrender!!!"

That didn't stop the flow of bullets shot downrange at him. Every 2-3 seconds a bullet would either hit the suit or hit the ground beside him. After 5 or so, he instinctively faced the other way and started running. Instinctive tears welled up again as started running. The Suits HUD started flashing a message, which Arun didn't pay any heed to.

...Charge Level- 78%...

"Position 3, he is headed your way, be alert" he spoke into the radio as he raised his rifle from the ground and slung it across his shoulder.

"Copy", came the reply buried in static.

He stood up and watched stoically as the faint image of suit disappeared over the edge of the valley.

16

The next day is noticeably easier on the lungs and moving around doesn't feel like a chore so much, Rohan is still in bed complaining of a heavy head, Arun and me, move over to Riya's room to plan out the activities that we have come for. A slight knock and the door flies open, Shilpa, effervescent as usual opens up and offers us some Chips that they have been munching on, while Riya looks confused pouring over some maps she borrowed from the reception last night.

"Hey, what's up?"

"Nothing much, trying to figure out the places that we would be going to" she replies without taking her eyes away from the map.

Shilpa butts in and makes the occasional joke about how Riya was never good with remembering any routes and she always had how she was terror behind the Scooty she drove in college.

"Can I take a look?" I offer

"Sure" she says gesturing me to take a seat right in front of her.

The map is laid flat and the extent of the mighty Himalayas is spread out right before me.

The centre point of the map is Leh with the other ranges spread beside it. I trace the road routes which go north and then turn east towards Kargil and to the south the routes that extend to Keylong and ultimately link up with Manali, the old and now famous routes to Khardung la and Nubra were to the north and the now famous Pangong Tso lake was to the South and close to the Aksai Chin region ceded to China during the Indo-Chinese war of 1962. The

Map was a mess to be honest it did not show a direct route to the place that we were supposed to go. The Hemis National Park. The biggest national park in the India also famous for the fact that here you could see the snow leopards or the Ghost cat. The cats have a reputation to be masters of stealth and often evading detection. The best time to see the Snow leopards is in the heavy winters when the cold temperatures force their prey down and of course predators follow their prey everywhere. With this unusual cold wave making the rounds this would be an opportunity to see the snow leopard, or at least that's what Rohan thought when he planned this whole trip. It was interesting to note that Rohan didn't know anything else about the Snow Leopards, neither was he a wild life enthusiast or as we had firmly established, even a photographer.

I look across to Riya who is now just as critically scanning the map as I was. I suggested that we take a Vehicle to the entrance of Hemis and then go on foot thereafter. Riya nodded with Agreement as she continued to look to the map

"But we want to go to some off-beat location" she exclaimed, "Not the same place where all the tourists go!"

I saw the map and was a little perplexed, the elevation and range were nothing that we had seen before, this wasn't Maharashtra, although I had done a lot of trekking and range climbing back in the home state but the terrain seemed steep and the altitude seemed demanding, I looked once at Arun and questioned my decision to bring him along. Shilpa was busy studying Arun for a long time; he caught on quickly and asked her a question midway during her gaze.

"Well?"

Shilpa seemed instantly taken aback by this retort, she waved her hands around to check if was really blind,
"Waving those hands isn't going to make me see you any more clearly"

Shilpa seemed even more intrigued by this.

"How did you know I was doing that?"

"People usually do when I stop them when they are staring at me."

"How did you know that??"

I let out a smile when I heard that question, Blind men are usually more aware of everything else that happens around them. It almost seems miraculous that they do that, it it's just basic observation

"Dude! You have some crazy sixth sense!"

"No, I don't, I just know how people react to me."

"Then tell me how does someone react to you?" she asked with the excitement of a child pulling a nearby pillow into her lap.

"Well, ever since we all met, I have never heard you be quiet for a long time, it obvious that silences make you uncomfortable. Right?"

Without waiting he continued,

"Also, when we were together alone for the first time, you didn't know how to react, since you probably haven't met anybody who is blind before. You wanted to say Hi! Or start talking right away, but were unaware of how to do that, since this is a new situation for you. You weren't sure, if saying something would be inappropriate or out of the ordinary, hence you were looking at me, wondering how to proceed."

Shilpa watched wide mouthed, as everything that Arun had said was spot on!

"Also, when I caught you in the act, you waved your hands just as a reflex to check if I really was blind, its normal it happens all the time with me. Don't feel sorry about it or anything, it's not your fault. It happens with everyone"

93

"Dude! You have some crazy sixth sense! She said again in the same voice.

Riya and I looked at each other, then at Shilpa and Arun and the room erupted with generous laughter. With Shilpa looking unsure of herself and Arun trying to control the loud snorting sound of his laugh. For whatever I thought of her earlier, Shilpa's heart seemed to be in the right place,

She was OK.

A knock on the door saw Rohan coming from our room looking to join in the fun. We presented him with the map and tried to explain how difficult the route would be to trek. He paid almost no attention to the whole deal and insisted that we first get some lunch before we did anything else. As we headed down to lunch, I wondered if the Hotel could arrange for the local specialities of the region rather than indulging in the regular fare that we eat all the time. Everyone liked the Idea when Tashi, our driver who was chatting up with another driver came along and asked us if we were feeling hearty enough to visit a Monastery close to Leh. Everyone seemed immediately on board and we settled into the Large SUV.

17

It's almost late afternoon, the sun has taken its toll, Arjun felt delirious while walking away from an invisible enemy that had chased him all day. No doubt the people were still in pursuit and he no longer had the will or the energy left to go on any further, he looked for a refuge, a Tree, a Rock, anything that could give him a few minutes of shade while he rested and contemplated the situation that he had gotten himself into, he spotted the side of a mountain that was shielded away from the Sun, he changed his direction while his legs felt heavy and his mouth was parched. He sat down with a thud still inside the ACE and let out his first breath of relief in the few hours that were spiked with danger. He felt his stomach growling and rued that there wasn't anything on him.

"Not even a Cigarette" he thought aloud as he looked around in the white desert that surrounded him, it had been snowing for some time, not a lot but enough to send the chill through the air and making him extremely uncomfortable. The HUD flashed again.

...Charge Level- 68%...

The suit is losing energy, he thought, we did have some battery problems but thought that they would be fixed by the time the Army gave the orders, which could have been quite a long time indeed. The batteries in the suit were a prototype and weighed little more than a quarter of the amount of the suit itself. The tech was secret, no one except the leadership knew, not even him. He remembered the amount of time he had spent looking forward to the end of this presentation when he could get back home and enjoy the fruits of his efforts, that wasn't going to happen now. He looked around for a bit and closed his eyes for a second, exhausted from the day, sleep slowly came over him and he drifted far and away from this place.

A small beeping sound repeating continuously woke him up. He opened his eyes slowly and blinked a few times. He tried getting up and failed. He realised he was in the suit.

"So it all wasn't a bad dream after all?"

He thought to himself, as he finally managed to get up. It was dark now, and the snow-capped mountains gleamed in the moonlight as he saw all around him. He looked at his arms and wondered if he should get out of the suit first and maybe if the people who were searching for him found him without the suit, they would be a bit calmer. The idea wasn't so bad, he wanted to get out of the suit to avoid looking like a threat and also, to relieve himself, Nature's calls needed answering. He started the exit protocol and the ACE started powering down, he removed his hands and legs from the large metal contraption and finally removed his helmet. He climbed out of the Machine and instantly felt the dry cold wind; he clenched his hands and wrapped them around his body while simultaneously trying to stretch out. He walked a few steps away, patted his pants to find a box of cigarettes and opened it to find a single cigarette and a lighter. He smiled to himself as he lit it. Every puff seemed heavenly and he felt safe. He got down to his business..

Somewhere in the mountains, not very far away.

"I do not have any target near my location, Repeat, No Target spotted" The radio came to life after many hours of silence

"I sent him in your direction, it's not possible, he should have been there hours ago."
"No Target, Repeat, No Target."

Well, he didn't go past me and he was headed for number 3's position, is it possible the Army caught up with him? He thought to himself.

"Number 1 come in,"

"Go for 1" came the reply, almost as a whisper.

"What's the situation at the base?"

"Base is filled with activity, the soldiers were dispatched some time ago, the top guy was wandering and speaking loudly into a radio, he seemed pretty pissed. That's all I could see."

"Copy."

The game isn't coming to the hunter; he should have been at number 3's position by now. He thought to himself.

"All team members, priority now is to locate the asset, withdraw from your positions and commence a search pattern. Search from last seen location and proceed grid wise. Avoid detection at all costs, even if it means giving up the asset. Maintain Radio silence till asset found. How Copy?

"Copy all" came the reply almost instantaneously.

"Number 2, What if we are detected?"

"If it's a large group, use your stealth to escape and if it's a small group, shoot them dead and proceed"

"Copy"

He turned around and looked at the direction he saw the ACE go in, holstered his radio and let out a grunt as he wore his backpack and started walking toward the ACE.

18

The breath taking view from the Thiksey Monastery almost falls short of words, the small kids rush up and down the monastery spinning the prayer wheels. The prayer wheels themselves are cylindrical with many inscriptions written on them in the mystical seeming Tibetan Script. Inside, I was told that there are mantras which are written and stored inside the wheel, spinning the wheel once is like reciting the mantra once. The Group merrily make their way inside and all of us are taken aback by the vibrant culture of this land. Arun walking with a little difficulty and I offer him my shoulder to grab on to, as we make our way to the top. The colourful prayer flags flutter in the wind and the sound catches Arun's attention. As he stops for a moment to take it all in. He asks me to move on ahead and says that we will catch up with me.

We move finally to the top of the monastery where the prayers are being held and we stop respectfully to observe the monks. Once it's all done, we move inside a large room to find a magnificent statue of the Buddha. It's beautiful. Even the chatty tourists who were quite loud outside seem spellbound and keep their mouths shut. Arun moves in, helped by a monk and without saying a word, sits down, we all follow suit and speak of nothing for what seems the longest time. Until, Shilpa speaks and reminds us that Lunch time will be over, we all smile and proceed down to the fare of the Yak butter tea and Noodles in some sort of Yak Milk gravy. Almost everyone we saw today was so happy. Even Arun doesn't ask to have a drink once we go back, that is not usually the case with him.

We come down to find Tashi waiting for us and asking us, how the trip was. When we all just smiled and got in the car, he got his answer. Rohan doesn't seem too annoyed with our presence anymore, or maybe he has just accepted that that this is the way things are going to go, Riya and Shilpa and Riya seemed to have raided the Monastery

Visitors Shop, Prayer Flags, wheels, bottle covers, phone purses and some things I don't know the purpose of but all of them make them seem pretty happy. We watch the children rush around the cars when they go by, shouting "Juley" with enthusiasm. Everyone's heart lifts. There is nothing like being welcome into someone else's home. The people and the countryside seem intent on keeping us in a good mood.

While waiting in the lobby for some free WI-Fi, it was finally discussed along with Tashi that the best would be to take a long drive into the mountains with some sort of sturdy SUV and avoid walking whenever possible because that would be too hard to do with Arun around, either we would have to leave him behind, or it would have slowed down the group by a lot. The group by now had taken a general liking to Arun and were not keen on leaving him behind. While everyone had originally thought of making the hike into the perching spots to see the ghost cat. It just seemed more appropriate to do it by car and avoid walking since the group also didn't have a lot of hiking or trekking experience. Between checking our mails and Shilpa's monster photo uploads, I managed to notice that Arun was missing and went up to the room to check on him. I opened the door and saw him sitting on a chair near the window. I removed my shirt and proceeded to ask a usually silent Arun about what was bugging him.

"I have it all wrong, I have been having it all wrong." he said, calmly

"What do you mean by that?" I put the T-shirt aside and walk over to him to probe further.

"I mean, I always regretted being blind and all the things I have ever done, the mad studying, the IIM, the big job, was because I was trying to be normal in a world where I didn't even understand what normal meant. Even my marriage, it was a way of showing off, and trying to declare to the people of the world how smart and how big I was, despite my handicap. I did wrong by that girl. I should have asked her how she felt and not considered that she would be happy because I

99

made a lot of money. "

I looked on, clasping my chin and listening.

"It's not some big revelation that was made to me in the Monastery or something like that. I have been thinking about it for some time. This change, gave me some clarity and some courage to speak out the words that were in my heart for a long time.

"I have not seen the world, I never will. It's almost paradoxical for a blind man to go see the sights. Anyone can see the irony in that sentence but this place, I feel free. I feel as if a large weight has been lifted from my heart. I want to go back and make amends, make every wrong thing right again. I want to go and talk to other people who feel like me and make them realise that Life is all about accepting what you are and not proving anything to anybody. If you want something, you should go after it but not because it would mean showing or proving something to someone who isn't going to be in your life anyway. Do things because you want to do them."

I look considerately towards Arun and put my hand on his shoulder. He doesn't cry or shake, he is calm as stone. He has his way. He understands what he needs to do.

"So, that means you are giving up drinking too right?"

"Oh! Fuck you! Absolutely not."

We both let out loud laughs and get back to doing whatever we were doing.

"I am really glad I came Vivek"

"I know Arun, I know."

19

The Sun is rising over the mountains; Arjun looks wearily towards them as he opens his eyes and spots the sun creeping up from the high peaks. The Suit kept him warm through the night.
"What a piece of machinery!"

His stomach growled from lack of food and for the first time in his life, he knew what true hunger meant. There was nothing that he could get his hands on, even the grass that would have otherwise been there was buried under the snow, he staggered to his feet and contemplated taking the suit off again. As soon as he was about to do that, he heard a shrill voice coming from his back, he moved his head, but the gargantuan nature of the suit, meant he had to turn his whole body. There was nothing there. He squinted and tried to see well. It was nothing.

He posited that it was the hunger playing tricks on him, the desolate and snow covered landscape only added to the surrealism of the place. Everything here was so alien, yet there was an undeniable sense of beauty in this place. He looked around and for quite some time, was left spellbound.

The same noise again, he looked again in its general direction,

"No, I definitely heard that one" he thought aloud to himself. As he took a few steps forward. He looked away into the snowy landscape, there seemed to be something moving in the rocks, the rocks made a sound as they tumbled down and at last he spotted something looked like a human figure. A single man sent out to apprehend him? No that would have been crazy, something is not right. He thought to himself.

"Let's see if the magnifier works..."

"ACE! Magnify"

A snapshot of the area in front of him appeared in a small screen in his HUD, the image showed him exactly what he thought, it was man in heavy camouflage, had it not been for the rocks tumbling down, he would never have made the distinction. A flurry of thoughts went through his head. He finally made the decision that it was best to be on the run until he can decide what was going on. He turned on his feet and started taking his first steps

"NO, wait. Something isn't right about this" he wondered the reason for the man's presence. He had made a lot of people unhappy, even if there was a search team sent after him, it would be extremely unlikely that that it would comprise of just one person. Maybe there are more and this one person is just an advance scout, or maybe it's possible that the others are taking up positions and trying to flank me? He contemplated all of these thoughts and decided he wasn't going to run any more. The hunger and the helplessness he felt meant that needed this episode to end one way or another. The best thing he decided was to hide out and wait for this person to come to him.

"Let him come then, I can decide what to do next, if he starts shooting then so be it. That's a risk I will have to take, otherwise I will never stop running and maybe a lucky bullet becomes the reason for my demise."

He looked around and saw a crevice and estimated that within 10 minutes, the man should be upon him and then he would figure out what to do next. As he lay hidden in the crevice, his palms started sweating up, the anticipation of what would happen next was making him uneasy and on edge.

His estimate was more or less right, in a short time, the man was in his field of view, he was wearing a white mask which only showed his eyes and mouth and slung a heavy looking gun from his right shoulder, even his gun was coloured and camouflaged. His boots and bag pack didn't resemble the ones the soldiers used back at the base. The man studied the place for a few minutes and started circling around.

Maybe special forces? Arjun thought to himself,
"They sent the special forces after me?" he whispered to himself.
"Shit! I am dead!"

The man looked around, kneeled and studied the patterns in the snow; jumping to his feet he suddenly seemed to have a sense of urgency. He started looking around nervously and unholstered his gun.

Chills ran down Arjun's spine. It was obvious that the man had figured out that he was here.

"Come out!" roared the man
"I know you are here! Come out, you have nothing to fear. I swear you will not be harmed"

Arjun's eyes teamed with nervous tears, he was too scared to move. This sudden change in heart of the people chasing him seemed improbable. His head tried to process the thoughts and came back empty.

The man noticed the trail that leads to the crevice; he looked dead centre and raised his gun.

"Come out of there, you have my word, you won't be harmed."

"Throw your gun away!" Arjun shouted from his hiding place.

"NO! What if your shoot me?"

"Well, what if you shoot me?" came the bewildered reply.

"Ok, here what we are going to do, I am going to raise my hands and so will you, we both raise our hands and you come out of there.. Is that ok?"

There was long silence, Arjun struggled with the decision, he made a face and fought back tears, the confidence in the man's voice, scared Arjun.

"OK, I am coming inside, if you don't have your hands up, I will have to shoot you."

"No wait! I am coming, raise up your hands. "

Arjun walked slowly and nervously, outside with his hands raised up.

The man also had his hands raised. They looked at each other for a few seconds. Silence passed between them, Arjun noticed how this man wasn't intimidated by the suit and seemed at ease. He took a step forward when the man stopped him.

"That's far enough, no need to come any further."

Arjun obeyed,

"Now, we have a situation, you see, both of us are standing with our hands in the air, none of us can put them down since we don't have any trust between us. So what don't you command your suit to disengage and I will put my Gun away, is that acceptable?"

"You out your gun away first!"

"No, I am just a normal man, with a gun, I have the higher risk" he said with a smile "If i put my gun down, you may simply shoot me. Also you are in a big metal box, you might even survive my bullets, I certainly won't survive yours"

His logic was sound; Arjun understood that behind that calm demeanour was a smart man.

"Ok, I am going to power down the Weapons system"

"ACE, power down weapons!"

-------------------------------Confirm Command----------------------------

"Yes"

-------------------------------Command confirmed--------------------------

"Very good, we are doing fine. Just fine. Now I am slowly going to lower my hands and put my Gun back on my shoulder. OK?"

The man put his back on his shoulder and lowered his guard. Arjun was finally calming down and the man spoke again.

"Now let's get you out of that thing"

"Fine" Arjun thanked his luck and let out a small thanks to the almighty. His ordeal was over and he was finally catching a break.

The man walked up to Arjun with a smile and raised his hands to help him out of the suit.

"Number 3 be advised, possibility of troops in your sector, remain hidden and ...."

He quickly turned off his radio. And put it away

"Wait, what was that?" Arjun asked

"Nothing, nothing just some chatter on the radio"

"So why did you turn it off?"

"It's nothing!" the man's reply was sterner than before and he concentrated on undoing the clamps near Arjun's neck.

"Wait, I want to see other soldiers and the Military Police" Arjun said as he pulled back.

"I already told you it was nothing, just come out first and then we can go join the others"

"So, OK, so let the others come, I am not coming out before I see some others"

The man's eyes burned as he heard Arjun say these words. Through the mask it was very difficult to see all of his expressions but Arjun realised that things were not right.

The man, raised his hands, turned around and as soon as Arjun relaxed, the masked man lunged for Arjun's throat. He held it in a vice grip as Arjun Grunted and made desperate attempts at breathing. The masked man's grip was tight and unrelenting; it felt as if every breath that Arjun took the grip got a little tighter. Still strapped to the ACE, Arjun moved around and tried desperately trying to shake him off but to no avail, he felt his head rushing with blood as his vision started darkening. Arjun swung wildly at the torso of the masked man and while every punch landed, the man simply grunted with pain but did not let go of his neck. The masked man smiled as he felt his prize within his reach as he saw the changing expressions on Arjun's face. With everything left in his body, Arjun raised his hand and hit one final time with every ounce of energy he had left. With a loud crack as metal met flesh, the masked man let out a blood curdling moan as he let go of Arjun's neck and his right hand grasped his chest. Arjun had broken the man's ribs and he stood writing in pain. Arjun was still down on all fours, coughing uncontrollably. Both men took a few moments to get back to their wits. While Arjun was still recovering, the masked man wobbled towards his gun which had been flung off during the scuffle. Extending his right hand with great difficulty, he lifted the gun which seemed to weigh a ton and with a moan, used his left hand to chamber a round. Arjun, seeing the turn of events, leapt to his feet and ordered the ACE to activate the weapons systems.

------------------------- Weapons System activated-------------------------

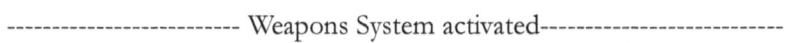

The masked man fired a round and missed wildly. Arjun took evasive action and moved out of the way, he held up his hands and squeezed his palm to fire off a round. The bullet found its mark and the masked man cried out. As he looked at his bleeding stomach, the sight of his own blood angered him and with a vengeance he reloaded his gun again, ignoring his pain and this time it impacted with the ACE. Ace's left arm had a noticeable dent. He reloaded again and before he could send another bullet downrange a scrambling Arjun rose to his feet only to slip off the edge he was standing on, he looked at the masked man and squeezed his palm again before slipping into the valley below. The bullet slightly grazed the right arm of the masked man but did no damage. Arjun screamed as he lost his balance. The ACE hit a rock as it fell and with Arjun still inside, his head was jolted forward because he masked man had managed to undo the straps on his neck. The rock impacted his helmet and Arjun was knocked unconscious.

Seeing Arjun fall into the valley the masked man fell to his knees in a combination of exhaustion and weakness. Hands shaking, he went for his Radio and opened up a channel..

"Team come in."
"I exchanged fire with the asset, I am wounded, lock on to my position, come soon, badly injured"
"Copy all, hold tight, we are on the way"

The masked man, lay down, grabbing his stomach, trying to put pressure and stop the bleeding, breathing heavily he waited for back up.

20

After having a heart to heart with Arun, I moved out of the room in a happy mood and felt like need to take a small walk around the hotel property, I saw Riya sitting in the lobby along with Rohan and Shilpa, looking as beautiful as ever. I stopped to exchange pleasantries and chat around, Rohan and Shilpa were headed back to the room and Riya seemed to look at me with a puzzling expression, till she asked,

"Are you going out?"
"Yeah, just a stroll"
"Ok, good. That's nice."
I looked smilingly at Shilpa who was giving me a very weird expression. I was trying to make sense of it till Rohan said,

"We can play cards, in the room, come on lets go up" said Rohan as he gulped down the fruit juice that was in front of him
There was another awkward silence. Riya was still looking at me till it finally struck me.

"Oh hey Riya, do you want to come along for the walk, it will just be a small one"

"Umm.. yeah, sure no problem, let's go."

I breathed a sigh a relief as I finally caught on to what I was supposed to do and didn't screw up the moment completely. Rohan looked as if he was just about to say something till Shilpa grabbed his arm and almost dragged him upstairs saying she wanted to teach the game to Arun. Poor Rohan, the expression on his face was really sad, but he wasn't becoming a third wheel today.

The small walk turned into a long walk and somewhere in between, we didn't realise when we started holding hands. I only realised it when I was moving away from a stall and felt Riya's hand pull me back, Walking through, I silently looked at our hands clasped together and then looked at her. She blushed and looked away smiling all the time. This was it, it was official, this was the best moment of my life. We walked and talked about a lot of things, I simply didn't know just holding hands could give me such joy. She didn't leave my hand the entire time. We walked and we walked, the markets were filled with beautiful things to behold and I didn't want the walk to end. We were finally done and by showing me the clock, Riya reminded me that it was time to head back and re-join the others.

We came up till the gardens of the hotels when a fleeting thought entered my mind, the lobby was a little far away and the lights of the gardens hadn't been turned on yet, or maybe the people forgot to turn it on, there were small shrubs on either side of the walkway and the moon was shining bright.

Is this the time? He thought to himself as slowly his heart started beating faster and faster. He stopped Riya by a slight tug and pulled her towards himself. Riya just smiled as he put his arms around her waist.

Riya playfully put her hand around Vivek's neck

"My my, you are awfully uncomfortable" as she felt him shake just a bit.

Vivek held his head a little closer as he felt his body getting warmer.

Riya, now committed to the moment leaned in to Vivek and planted her lips on his. Both locked their lips passionately and hugged each other tight. When they let go after what seemed an eternity, both of their hearts were beating so fast, they could hardly believe it. They looked lovingly into each other's eyes and held hands again to move into the Hotel.

"That was the happiest moment of my life" he said to Riya as they parted ways to go to their rooms

Vivek strolled in to Arun reading a book and without saying a word crashed into bed next to him.

"So! It happened didn't it?"

"Oh shut up!"

"What happened?" Rohan enquired as he came out of the Washroom.

"Nothing Rohan, Arun is being his obnoxious self" I said as quickly as I could.

The next day, we all left early and before the sun rose to cover as much distance as we could to make sure that we could have maximum sunlight on the bad roads, the roads in and out of Leh were ok, but Tashi had warned us that it could turn rough later on.

Tashi was jovial and about the same age as us, a little older maybe. He cracked jokes and laughed at quite a few of ours, he played some "hit" Ladkahi Songs on full blast and we danced in our own unique ways inside the car, much to the amusement of the locals who passed us by. It was safe to say, that all of us, were having a good time. Even Rohan had opened up and was comfortable that I and Riya were growing closer. We stopped at a few places where Tashi told us were places of some importance and truth being told, we needed the break to stretch out our limbs. We met an old lady on one of the stops, who seemed delighted to meet us. She neither spoke a word of English or Hindi and we didn't speak a word of Ladkahi except "Juley", which was all that we needed to understand each other apparently. We ended up making funny faces at each other and shared a few energy bars that we were carrying, both of us departed with smiles. We waved to some of the Army trucks from the car by and were met with smiles and waves in return. After around 4 hours of driving, a small side road appeared. Tashi told us that the route was going to get especially bumpy and we should hold on to something. Negotiating the small roads was becoming tricky and the music, laughter and cacophony stopped. Tashi expertly guided the car through the nooks, crannies and potholes to get us through to the other side. With a pat on Tashi's back, Rohan commended his driving skills which Tashi seemed very proud about and as soon as a patch of firm road appeared, Tashi picked up some speed. The Black rock of mountain on our left was restricting with patches of snow just beginning to form but the view to our right was breath taking! It had just started snowing and the light snow descended from the sky much to the delight of Shilpa who promptly got her camera out and started clicking pictures. Riya looked at me and smiled while I covered my eyes and let out a smile. The mood lightened up again, Tashi put the music on again and Rohan turned it up on full blast rudely awakening a sleeping Arun.

"What? What's happening?!"

"Arun! Did you sleep through that?" asked an astonished Shilpa

"Sleep through what?"

"The bloody road from hell! What else?"

"What can I say? Rocking of any kind puts me to sleep"

"Damn dude!"

"Wait till you see me in the trains, you won't believe what happens...."

Everyone jerked forward, as the jarring sound of the screeching brakes mixed with a crashing sound of the windscreen braking took the breath out of everyone. Shilpa and Arun almost fell of their seats; Rohan would have impacted the wind shield if not for his seat belt. Tashi was also recovering, noticeably in pain as fragments of the wind shield lay in both their laps and mixed in with their shirts. I looked at Riya as she was palming her head which impacted the middle seats headrest. I opened the door of the vehicle to better help the others when I realised my left hand seemed to have a small injury, the skid marks on the road conveyed instantly it was a very unpleasant stop, I moved around and saw the car's front end deeply dented and a sliver of metal stuck out of the field of view. I came around for a better look, resting right on the road, what was that?

"Is that? Is that a man?"

21

Project Trident-

Colonel Brar paced around the office as soldiers were given orders and the entire base was abuzz with activity. The office phone rang and the Colonel picked it up.

"Sir, there is an urgent call from Brigadier Bakshi"

"Put him through"

"Brar, what is the situation report?" asked a scruffy voice

"Until now the fugitive is on the run and we currently do not know of his whereabouts."

"How did this happen? I read the report which was compiled but I want to hear it from you. "

"Once the suit was placed for demonstration, the Fugitive got in it, he shot a Captain and then a soldier and when we tried to disarm him, he resisted capture and fled the scene."

"It's the same thing in the report; I want to know what happened, not what is in the report."

"Sir, currently we do not have an idea of what is happening, or why the Fugitive did what he did. What we do know is that 2 soldiers are dead and we need to find this person, before he does something else."

"It was a presentation wasn't it? How did you turn it into a demonstration?"

"I wanted to know if the machine could be used for active service now, not years later."

"So you bypassed me and went about ordering Accurate technologies to deliver the machine?"

"That's right Sir.

"Colonel, we aren't at War and Project Trident is a secret that we have maintained for a long time, your distinguished service has gotten you to this point where you are privy to secrets and plans most in the Service aren't. The Demonstration was supposed to take place in a confined area. By doing this, you have jeopardised the Project. If the news or any other agency catches wind of this, you will have single handedly destroyed our entire Project. "

"We shall catch him before that happens and bring him to justice before any of that can happen Sir."

"What's his name again? The fugitive?"

"Arjun Joshi."

"For your sake and for the sake of the security of the Nation, I hope you do."

A little uneasiness weighed over him. He knew, he was the reason that 2 soldiers are dead. They might have been killed by another but he was the one who put them in that situation.

A knock on his door, there was a soldier standing outside. Impatient to barge in.

"Sir" he said as he stormed in.

"There is something on the radio, two of our soldiers in the patrol team were found dead and there is some encoded message on the Radio's we can't determine."

The Colonel looked wide eyed as he finally remembered he was not the phone,

"Sir, there is some development I will speak to you later."

The Colonel rushed from his office to the radio room,

"What's happening" the Colonel said with urgency in his voice.

"Sir, 2 of our soldiers who had split up from the main group to conduct the combing operations, were just spotted dead by the main group, they radioed it in. I can't say for sure, but they seem to be around 40km's from here. They say they also picked up some weak radio signals"

"Are they still on the Radio?"

"Yes Sir."

"Connect me now."

"This is Hades, come in Apollo"

"Go ahead Hades."

"What is the radio Chatter you are hearing?"

"Not much, the only thing we could make out was "Asset", the message certainly wasn't being broadcast on our frequencies and we only found about them when we were searching all the bands to see if Joshi was doing anything"

The Colonel's eyes went red with anger.

"This was pre planned! They wanted the ACE to come here. He

wanted to leave with it! Joshi must have known all along and played us for a fool, that Traitor!"

"Sir?"

"Don't you see? This was a way of using that Joshi as a means of getting the suit out of our hands! That Joshi! So innocently he said, I am not qualified to operate it, I don't know how to operate it."

"So his whole idea was to make a run with the machine?"

"Damn right! That Traitor! Get me the Brigadier on the phone again, we need to have a talk, in the meanwhile I want you to alert the serving units in the area and inform them to extend us all the support they can give to Apollo and intensify the search for him he must be caught at the earliest. Issue the order, either apprehend him or shoot him dead, either way I want that suit back!"

"But Sir! That will mean telling them about what happened here, our cover will be blown"

"Right now, it is more important to stop that man and retrieving our suit."

As the Colonel stormed out of the room the confused radio team looked at each other and started imagining the implications of what the Colonel had just said. A traitor was just here at their base, he fooled them and ran off with a priceless piece of technology and if the tech fell into the wrong hands, there is no telling what would happen. They went back to their Radio sets and relayed the orders further. The hunt had begun.

22

Vivek traversed the small distance between him and the large metal object. He instinctively looked up to see where it had come from. It didn't make sense, where did it fall out of? He made his approach slow and cautiously. Rohan unbuckled himself and came out of the car. He crept up slowly behind Vivek. They made it to the base of the object till they saw a man's face, his eyes were shut and he had a blank expression. They looked up together in wonder trying to figure out where it came from. Small snowflakes continued to fall at an even pace, unperturbed by the change of events. Rohan asked Vivek, if the man was unconscious because the car hit him? Vivek looked long and hard but couldn't come up with anything. He suggested that Rohan have a look in the car and he would check out this man here. Tashi was already out and making sure that the girls and Arun was OK. Only Arun seemed severely rattled and Shilpa and Riya were trying to make sure that he was getting water and he seemed normal. Vivek wanted to go to him but his curiosity was getting the better of him. He slowly sidestepped and made it to the man's face. He seemed dead. His eyes were closed and no sign of life seemed apparent on his face.

He thought of delaying anything to do with the man before all of his mates were OK and they made sure that there was no more danger left in the immediate vicinity. He helped Arun around and explained to him that a man in metal had apparently fallen on the car and it seemed that was the reason for the large impact.

"Just our luck eh?" Arun sure knew to smile even in the worst of circumstances.

"Riya, Shilpa are you fine?"

Both of them nodded in the positive, they only scratches, nothing severe, Riya was still nursing the hit she got but seemed OK"

Rohan by now, was standing right next to the metal box when he got suddenly spooked and came running towards Vivek..

"It's not dead!" he shouted.

Everyone became alert again. Vivek moved slowly back to the place that the man was lying and decided to give it another look through. The eyes slowed some sign of movement along with the nose, he held his hand close to the nose of the man to check if he was still breathing.

"Water!"

"Get me some water!" he shouted, he is alive!

Tashi came with a bottle and Vivek took a hand full and gently sprinkled it over the man's face. After 2 sprays, the man slowly started opening his eyes and Vivek's fear that that they had killed him was alleviated.

"Hey. That's it. Slowly, Slowly"

Arjun's eyes opened slowly, a little blurry at first, there was someone crouching over his face and his face felt moist. In an instant he remembered the events just before everything went black. Arjun jumped to his feet, pushing away Vivek and Tashi in the process and pointing his arms toward towards them. Seeing the man on the ground encased in Metal was bad enough, but now seeing a giant stand up and threaten them seemed entirely different.

"Who are you, what do you want?" cried a bewildered Arjun.

"Woah! Woah! Woah! Easy, We didnt do anything !"

Rohan now stood firmly behind Vivek and did not speak at all. He might as well have grabbed his shirt like a little boy. Vivek was by no means at ease, his entire body shook and he didn't know what would happen next.

Words weren't exchanged between the two as they peered into each other's eyes, standing barely 2 feet apart, Arjun didn't budge from his position and neither did Vivek lower his arms. The silence wasn't helping. While Rohan stood behind Vivek, Tashi was frozen just next to the car along with Riya, Shilpa and Arun. Arun didn't have a clue about what was going on and was the most spooked of anybody.

Arjun moved his hands around, breathing a little heavily and still in alert mode, Asked slowly with a hint of nervousness in his voice.

"Who are you?"

"Sorry?" Vivek seemed astonished by the question, but didn't want him to repeat.

"I am Vivek, and this is Tashi our driver, Shilpa, Arun and Riya, we are all just friends."

"Just friends?"

"The thought of Riya as just friends crossed Vivek's mind and made him smile a bit but he repeated"

"Just friends, we were on our way for a trip, when we crashed into you, or you crashed into us we don't know"

So you were not sent by anybody?"

"No No, not sent by anybody or anyone"

Arjun seemed to believe him, he out his hands down and came out of his defensive position. As soon as he did that, a wave of relief went through everyone else. They didn't even know what was happening to them, now this metal man appears out of nowhere, their car is possibly damaged, and they are in the wilderness without any support.

"Do you have anything to eat?" asked Arjun

The request seemed strange to Vivek but Arjun was absolutely famished and would have gulped down anything given to him.

"We have some chocolate and energy bars."

"Can I have them?"

"Sure" He motioned to Rohan to go the bars, Rohan was still almost mute and this whole episode hadn't done much to lift his spirits, he was still unsure of the behemoth in front of him, as is natural, his fear was founded and it would be foolish not to experience fear. Riya and Shilpa sat close to Arun while Tashi, remained close to the driver's seat. Everyone almost assumed that the man in front of them was dangerous. Arjun looked hard at Vivek, who seemed to be studying him.

"It's a suit! It's Armour"

"What is it for?"

"I am sorry but I can't reveal that."

"Ok. Fine, here, you go, some chocolate for you"

Arjun came closer and the size of the suit really made the others uncomfortable. Arjun removed his hands and clasped the bars of chocolate in Vivek's hands. Eating with frenzy, he never took his eye off the group and remained suspicious of them. Life has taken such a weird turn. He thought quietly to himself as he relished the bars with the speed of a 5 year old.

Arjun then looked at his HUD again, battery level was at 40%.

"You are on the run aren't you?"

"No, not really"Vivek replied, a little flustered

Rohan whispered into Vivek's ear very discreetly, "Maybe asking him if he is an escaped criminal isn't the best way to start, he may kill us all, he hasn't so far."

"No, I am not a criminal, well now anyway, since everyone will soon know me as a...."

"As a what?"

"Forget it I don't want to get into it." He replied, with frustration on his face,

"Does anyone have a phone? He asked excitedly, his nature changing again!"

"Yeah, but we are out of the coverage zone."

"Damn! I really needed to make a call!"

"What's your name?"

"Arjun"

"Hi, Arjun I introduced myself earlier but I am not quite sure you will remember, so just in that case, I am Vivek".

"I am just constantly on edge, the last day has been very eventful for me and i don't know what to think of."

"Are you in the Army?" Vivek asked, looking suspiciously at his hair, they certainly didn't have a short cut.

"No, I am not in the Army!"

"Then what are you doing here?"

"I can't answer that question"

Vivek was getting ever so suspicious about his Man and his purpose here, it had been an hour and soon, it would be dark, Darkness starts quickly in the mountains, and they certainly weren't prepared for a night in the mountains in this weather. Arjun sat on one side, while Vivek could see the rest, chatting away, and looking incredibly scared, he called for Tashi, who refused to budge out of the car. Ultimately Vivek went up to him and asked coolly.

"Can we get out of here?"

"NO, the engine has some problem, won't start"

"What do you think is the problem?"

"I don't know, the bonnet is dented pretty badly from the impact, I can't even lift it up to see what's wrong."

"So we are stuck? Think of something, we have girls with us"

"Sir, I didn't plan for this, the only thing we can do is wait for the army or any other car coming this way for help."

"How long will that take?"

"This is a non-inhabited area; it's not even too close to the border, so there is no reason for anyone to patrol this wilderness"

"So you are basically saying, it would take a while, before we are declared missing."

"It could take more than a week"

"Damn it! Hey what about the people at the base camp of the village that we are going?"

"They don't know we are coming, it's just a village of about 90 people, they set up everything as soon as we go there."

"So, we are stuck here."

"Pretty much."

Vivek walked back with the bad news to his group and he saw their faces drop. This was bad, real bad. Their thirst for an off-beat adventure had brought them to the brink of something extremely dangerous.

"So the Bonnet's bent you say?" Arun inquired

"Yeah."

"Help me up" Vivek helped him up to his feet

"What's up buddy?" Vivek enquired

"Hey you, the man who fell on us!"

23

"What do we do about Number 3?"

"He is too far gone, more than 20 minutes in this weather with a stomach wound, he is dead already. Also, even if we could reach him and he was alive, what do you think we can do for him? Set up an IV line, stitch the wound and give him a blood transfusion?"

"Shouldn't we take him back?"

Number 2 looked confused and started at his colleague.

"I mean, if the Indian's find him, it will be a bit of a bother wont it?"

"You just killed 2 soldiers; do you not think that would have been reason enough for the Indians to come after you? You are as stupid as you look."

"I mean, if he is found they will look for us too"

"Even if he is found there is nothing on him linking him to us, or who we represent. Yes, there is the possibility that they will come looking for us but in all probability by the time they reach number 3, the snow would have covered him up and when it thaws, whenever that it, they may or may not discover the body. So in any case, it doesn't matter. What matters now is the asset. It's what we came here for. Don't forget that.

The two made their way over ice filled grounds and mountains. Their training had turned them into almost supermen at this altitude their stamina, their resolve and their aloofness were all qualities they were selected for, from the best battalions from the country, they were here to pay their dues, perform their duty for their nation. They didn't have a bond, after all, you can't expect tigers to share territory and work together. Their ferocity was legendary and they existed only in myth. The Indian Soldiers would often talk about a mountain spirit, a spirit which played mischief with them. Often confusing the patrols by destroying markers, stealing food from their camps, throwing rocks from above. The soldiers would swear and hurl rocks from the mountains, they recited prayers and tied prayer flags to ward off the evil spirits but they would always disappear the next time they would come again to the same place.

The mountain spirit was hunting today and it wasn't alone. Trained for sabotage, subterfuge, nearly all types of weapons and how to be almost invisible, the men simply known as "Team A", didn't exist on paper and were often on the wrong side of the border, keeping a close watch on the enemy. In a document sitting somewhere in the capital, their names, known only by a few select generals was all that remained of their identity. The people and the party came first. Individualism didn't matter among them but loyalty and absolute obedience did, a paradox of human behaviour

A relic of the lone wolf ideology, there would always be one stationed somewhere inside the border, today there were 3. The lone wolves roamed the terrain, hiding, waiting and collecting information. It was risky, but they were masters of their craft and none were caught or even detected in the 15 years they had operated. The Kargil conflict, now famous for its massive intelligence failure, didn't teach the Indians much. They still relied on antiquated ways of intelligence gathering; asking Villagers and using information from Soldiers without doing most of the leg work themselves. Their satellites were the best in remote detection in the world but they couldn't use them easily because to access them was another bureaucratic nightmare. They were more vigilant than before but they couldn't cover every place, they couldn't plug all the holes. What if these holes could be exploited? What if it was possible to always keep an operative behind enemy lines? What if it was possible to have highly trained soldiers always available at a moment's notice to hit the enemy hard before even a single shot was fired from beyond the border?. They could never be caught, the Cyanide made sure that the Soldiers ended their life before that and the special training ensured that their chances of them being caught we so small, that they could easily ignore that possibility.

While the Military base was shrouded in secrecy, the ACE showing up was more of a surprise. The Indians thought that keeping the ACE tests and the base with a skeletal staff and close to the border would avoid any eyebrows. The masked men already knew something fishy was going on there. While the Indians thought they would remain invisible by not having a large staff, an elaborate base and a non-existent security detail, it backfired. They hadn't factored in these hunters. It was sheer luck that Number 1 was patrolling this sector and the base caught his eye. There was intelligence that the Indians were developing an alternate fighting system but up till now they didn't have solid leads. The plan was born; take it back at any cost, except being discovered.

Number 1 updated the duo.

"Another Kilometre and we should be close to the asset"

"The readings show that number 3 is dead, it's been over an hour now I told you we would never make it in time"

"Hey, I just thought 3men would be better than 2, that's all. After all we are taking on a big metal beast. If it could injure and kill Number 3 that means it's not something that we can take lightly."

"I have that in mind. We aren't going to take it down by brute force, that's not possible; we need to trick it into submission."

"Beyond this next boulder, we should pick up his trail again. Let's hope we are luckier."

Number 2 moved closer and maneuvered around the boulder and stopped dead in his tracks, he held up a closed fist and signalled Number 1 to stop. He did and crouched down. Number 2 held up 6 fingers and a "C" sign and then 1 finger and joined his thumbs together.

This meant simply that there were 6 civilians he could see and the asset was among them. This complicated matters, the duo didn't expect to find the Asset so close to the location of 3. They had assumed he had simply picked himself up and run away. These civilians aren't supposed to be here as well. Are they in some way related to the incidents that have been happening? He climbed down from the boulder and looked straight at 1.

"How do we proceed from here?"

"Pincer move."

"I will move quickly to the other side and flank them from the back, they aren't expecting anybody at the moment and why the Civilians are here is unclear."

"Do we shoot the Civilians?"

"No, not now at least, if we shoot the civilians, the asset could run again. That would mean another chase, I don't want that. Plus, we don't want to leave such a large profile; you have already killed 2 soldiers. Six Civilians is a large number and will make a large wake and attract unwanted attention. Let's not kill anybody at this point, plenty of time for that later"

Number 1 nodded his head in agreement. Number 2 quickly disappeared behind the mountain and 1 took his position, he crouched and finally lay flat on the ground, the Telescopic sight revealed all the players.

24

"You crashed into us and now we are stranded here, this is your fault." Arun hadn't raised his voice or seem angry; he said it as a simple matter of a fact.

"It's not my fault!"

"Sure it is."

"I don't owe you any explanations and what are you looking at?"

"I'm blind genius or does that suit not tell you already?"

"Oh, I am sorry."

"Help us get out."

Tashi stood by, not uttering a word and now terrified after what Arun had said, he didn't have an idea if this was going to help them or did Arun's choice of words just make him angry. In that case, this was bad news. Tashi slowly moved behind the bonnet, close to the driver's seat.

"I need to get out of here and continue"

"You can't just leave us here! Where are we supposed to go? What are we supposed to do?"

"I don't care! It's not my problem"

Vivek stepped in,
"Hey, Can you help us with the bonnet of the car?"

"With what?"

"The bonnet. When you fell the bonnet it got depressed and now is in a place that we can't open it to see what's wrong with the engine. If you can open it, maybe we will be able to get the engine started."

That seemed reasonable, He could try that.

"Sure, I can try."

Arjun moved to the car and Tashi stood frozen as ever. With a slow action, Arjun gripped the deformed bonnet and started pulling. The force of the pull was so much that the car started getting pulled along with attached bonnet. Arjun then placed one foot on the car and pulled again on tight tugs, the entire bonnet came out, much to the horror of Tashi, who seemed mostly reserved and afraid. His anger boiled and finally he lashed out.

"You idiot! First you collide with us and now you broke my car's bonnet!"

"I was just trying to put it back into shape."

"But who told you to rip it off!"

"I didn't know the bonnet was so weak!"

"Weak? What weak? It's not weak! You broke it by putting too much force! Who is going to pay for this?"

"Don't you have insurance?" the simple reply was enough to incite a smile or two in the people sitting nearby.

"What are you smiling about?"

"He does have a point" said Rohan.
"The Insurance will cover it don't worry about it."

"I give you all a ride in my car! I talk about my life with you and this is how you repay me, you siding with the person because of whom the accident happened? Not to mention, I wouldn't even have come on this route if not for your relentless insistence!"

"Tashi chill! The insurance will cover it, it's a car, Accidents will happen! Also, you took good money for coming on an offbeat route; you didn't do it for charity. "

"What am I supposed to write on the cause of the accident? Giant metal man fell out of the sky and damaged the car?"

Tashi and Rohan went at till for some time, with Rohan trying to convince an irate Tashi that things would get sorted out, what was important was to get the car running again and for them to get out of this situation. You can threaten a man but the moment you threaten his livelihood, you will have trouble, men have the ability to stand up to the highest of dangers when it comes a question of surviving.

Vivek looked over at Riya and Shilpa; both wore expressions of grim and didn't quite know how to react to the situation in front of them. Arun seemed to wearing an expression of frustration and looked trapped. Rohan on the other hand, stepped up completely and forgot about the whole man in the suit, trying to calm Tashi down and help us get back on the road.

"Ok, Ok. Fine, I will try and fix this and once we get back, we will have to talk about the damages,"

"Great Tashi, now we can get back on the road again, we will figure this out once we get back to Leh"

Tashi let out a sigh of grief as he looked at the open engine without a hood and started fumbling around with the engine to make it start as Rohan looked on hands folded. Shilpa got up and simply opened the car door and seated herself inside, in a few minutes, she had dozed off. The stress is what must have been too much for her., as she. Riya sat next to Arun and both of them started talking about Fate and how it led them here. To see all of them talking the way they did, unnerved Vivek a bit, He had not expected the reactions to be in this case, quite grounded.

Vivek wasn't done with Arjun. He walked over again and tried looking as comfortable as possible, he sat down next to him and pulled a cigarette out of his pocket and lit it. Arjun flipped instantly and looked on, Vivek noticed it. A smokers desire.

"He must be a heavy smoker to be exited quite so easily." He thought.

Arjun caught him looking and he instantly looked away.

"Want one?" He enquired

"No Thanks" It took everything Arjun had say no, lighting one up would mean getting out of the suit. It was his safe haven at this point. There was no way he was going to come out of that.

Everyone settled down, waiting for the next thing to do.

The wind was starting to pick up, the travellers kept to their own and didn't engage in much discussion but the highlight of the day had quickly gone from a Giant metal object crashing into them, to Tashi trying to pick a fight with a seemingly superhuman opponent.

He seemed content for now, tending to the engine. Talking to himself and working laboriously for quite some time.

"This should do it."

Tashi beamed and that got everyone's attention. Vivek got up and walked towards the car and so did Riya and Arun. They all gathered around the car as Tashi turned the keys and hoped to hear the engine come to life. Everyone hoped that the faint sound that the motor made as Tashi turned the keys would culminate in the engine starting. After 4 attempts, Tashi gave up and came back in front of the vehicle.

Vivek came close to Riya and tried taking her hand. She flinched ever so slightly; the message seemed unclear at first. Arun too, seemed defensive. All of them weren't freaking out but they were all definitely on edge. He couldn't blame them; the day had been eventful to say the least. Vivek looked again at the man in his metal contraption, he had nodded off. Why wasn't he running again? What was keeping him here? Tashi tried turning the keys again and the loud misfire of the engine woke up the soundly sleeping man.

His eyes had panic in them, he too seemed traumatised, it wasn't a place he was comfortable in. Vivek went up to him and asked him pretty plainly why he wasn't leaving?

"Where would I go?"

That was all he needed to know, he was on the run for sure.

Just then, Tashi asked everyone to help him reverse the car and change the direction the car was facing, he thought the incline would help them, if the car needed a running start. Everyone got together and pushed the car in position, Tashi put the car in the second gear and proclaimed that this was the only way we could start the car now. Shilpa who was still inside the car had gone awfully silent and refused to come out, even to push. While Vivek tried calling her out, Rohan simply signalled to let her be. Arjun volunteered to push having his strength would mean easier pushing, it would have been a breeze, or so everyone thought, except for Tashi, who didn't want Arjun's hands on his car again. Being in a fix, he finally agreed after a letting his displeasure quite openly known.

Everyone got together and heaved, the car started moving, with frequent jerks, Tashi was trying to jump the engine back to life. For about 500 meters they pushed, again and again, they negotiated a difficult bend and when they came to the other side, the pushing started again. Just at the edge of hope, when they thought the car would be stranded. The Engine roared and came back to life. Everyone celebrated with high pitched squeals and high fives. Rohan opened the door to get in and that's when Tashi asked him to wait a bit, he wanted to run the engines for a bit and make sure the car had warmed up appropriately. Shilpa was wearing a smile now, as she looked towards Vivek.

"Can we just please get out of this place now?" Arun said as she shook his hands around which brought smiles back to everyone's faces.

In the laughs and high-fives Vivek looked at Arjun, he was looking happy, perhaps because this went so well. He hadn't spoken to anyone else and since it was time to leave, he decided that they needed to talk.

"So, we will be heading back now."

"Yeah, looks that way"

"Is there something we can do for you?"

Tashi offered his piece of unsolicited advice about turning him into the nearest police station and continued to mumble something below his breath.

"It won't be a bad idea, turning myself in, I have been trying to do just that" said, dropping his face a little

While Vivek listened, he thought to himself, how do you tell the authorities that a 9 foot tall metal man was on the loose? It would have sounded crazy. Vivek thought looking to the valley below.

"Can I have a cigarette?" came the request out of the blue.

"I knew you smoked! Looking at the way you saw me when I was lighting one up."

Vivek went for his backpack inside the car, he grabbed the pack from inside and made his way back opening the pack and taking out a single cigarette.

"Can you light it?"

Vivek smiled as he lit the cigarette and held it out.

Arjun wrestled his hand out of the restraints and reached out to receive it.

Riya, who had been standing just behind them, froze.

"Guys..." She said nervously

25

"He is a traitor and he made fools out of all of us. We need to talk to the others right now and confirm their situations"

"We don't break protocol just yet."

"What if the others are deceived?"

"They aren't, we haven't lost touch with them and they are proceeding as planned."

"Sir, we need to find out if the traitor had accomplices."

"You are awfully concerned about this Brar. Are you sure he bolted and he is a traitor or a collaborator? "

"With due respect Sir; I am not sure you understand the gravity of this situation"

"Careful now Brar, you have yourself to blame for this fiasco, or maybe when it turns into one"

"Sir, I have already informed the regular units in the area to comb the valleys, they won't leave a stone unturned, we also, have some new information."

"What's that?"

"Apparently, there were some transmissions picked up in the area, which refereed to the ACE as an asset"

There was a long pause on the other side.

"You are sure of this? That's what the message says?"

"No, we only picked up a small part, and this is how we know that Joshi is fleeing possibly to link up with someone."

"How much did you intercept?"

"Not much Sir, but what we did intercept, shows a clear relation, it can't be anything else."

"The basic idea of this entire operation was to simply test the readiness of the entire program and to see how far along it has reached. You have made sure of a breach, but here let me ask you think question, you saw the tech first hand. How is it?"

"It's Magnificent"

"That's all I want to know."

Colonel Brar, looked uneasy, there was truth in his statement, there was no mistaking it. The Ace had been without a doubt the best fighting machine he had ever seen, he fumbled about and brushed the papers on his desk. He remembered his time in the war, he remembered the blood but mostly he remembered dying soldiers and those unfortunate enough to have their youth taken away from them and then presented to the world as half martyrs, those fortune enough to sacrifice all they had for their country but only to have disability given to them in return. If only something like this was available back then, he thought. Brigadier Bakshi was not in the services much longer than Brar was, in fact, he had recently been promoted. He didn't like him very much but protocol dictates that a superior rank must be saluted and called Sir. He thought of him, more as a politician than an army man. The only reason he put up with so much of what he hated about him, was his dedication to Project Trident.

Project Trident was the most secretive project that was ever run by the armed forces, being tapped to serve in it was personally quite gratifying to the Colonel. He had been kept under check for so long, that he was almost ready resign his commission, the only thing that kept him going as his dedication to this country and the belief that sometimes, even though unpleasant, steps would have to be taken to ensure the greater good . He thought about this for a while, re arranging his table when his attention was drawn to his office door. It was a Lieutenant who had been posted on the recommendation of Bakshi, since the order came from Bakshi, it was no surprise that there was always a permanent winter between them.

"May I come in Sir?"

Brar carried on looking at his table and arranging things, ignoring him.

"Sir, may I come in"

"Come in" Brar replied while staring him unapologetic about the earlier snub.

"Sir, there are some angles that we have previously not considered"

"Really?, Tell me 'Lieutenant' what have all the other officers missed that you haven't?"

"Sir, after the incident I went in to the clinic, I looked at Captain Thevar and the other Jawan, more specifically at their wounds"

"You dared to touch the body of a fallen soldier?" Colonel Brar said, widening his gaze

"If I may Sir,"

"How dare you? Is that what is taught in the Academy now? To go around poke your nose into dead soldiers corpses?"

"Sir the wounds that the soldiers have don't match up" he said, cutting him off before he could go on any further.

"What? What do you mean by that?"

"Sir, you asked him what kind of bullets the suit fired, he said 25 caliber, to which you asked him, why did they use such an odd number"

Brar remembered something of the exchange that took place between Arjun and himself.

"Go on, what's your point?"

"The point is that a 25 caliber at such a close range would have taken his head off clean Sir. And even if there was muzzling we would still have heard of something resembling a gun shot, we didn't hear anything at all. "

"We did hear the gunshot later on, when the Jawan died"

"There was firing all along, how can be sure that the sound of the Gunshot emanated from the suit or that Joshi fired it? I have certainly never heard the suit fire before and neither have you, so how can we be sure that it's the suit that fired when we don't know what the firing sounds like?"

Brar looked a little uneasy, his mind pondered the possibilities

"What else came to your mind?"

"I don't think Joshi fired at all"

"Then how are two soldiers dead?"

"I am not sure Sir but the only logical conclusion is that someone else must have shot them. From the base would have been impossible but from outside, there is a possibility that we have missed that approach and with it perhaps our window"

The thought suddenly hit Brar head like a speeding truck. The logic was sound and the conclusion seemed to follow the premise. He looked at the young Lieutenant and rocked slightly in his Chair. He brought his fist to his chin and said.

"All of your reasoning only implies that the killing shots were not from Joshi. We don't know if they were from another projectile launcher in the suit that we don't know of. It also doesn't completely absolve him from being part of a wider strategy to escape with a valuable piece of technology that has hundreds of crores invested in it"

"Under the circumstances Sir,"

Brar raised up his hand to silence him.

"How many have you told about this so called theory of yours?"

"At present, only you Sir."

"Good, you will at the present time, refrain from engaging in mental jousting with any other personnel in this base. You will not engage in further discussion about his particular topic, unless you are asked to by me, specifically. Those are my orders are present time. Is that understood?"

"Yes Sir" he said standing in attention.

"Dismissed".

26

It took a while for everyone to notice, Vivek was the closet, standing next to Arjun. Rohan froze in his tracks while Tashi, Arun and Shilpa were too far to notice and the sound of the engine was drowning out every other sound.

"Make no quick movements!" Riya obeyed

He walked inch by inch closer with Riya in front. He hid himself well behind her. It wasn't until they were close enough that Vivek noticed the gun to the back of Riya's head and Arjun noticed what he was wearing.

Arjun's expression went blank.

"I shot this man!" He thought to himself.

"How is he still walking? How did he make it this far down? Was he wearing a vest? No, I saw blood pouring down. How can it be?"

"Both of you there, move back" said the main in a slight accent.

Arjun instantly recognised the voice, it wasn't the same man. The other man's voice wasn't as deep as this one's. Vivek remained motionless with the cigarette still in his hands, trying hard to figure out if he was dreaming. The man crept up to them as they took steps backwards; He held Riya's hair in a tight grip, pulling at it every now and then to make sure she was in his control. Tashi looked back in the rear view mirror and instinctively turned around. A bullet whizzed past his head and hit the rear view mirror. Tashi jumped in his seat while letting out a small shriek. Instantly Shilpa and Arun were shocked by the discharge of the Weapon and the mirror breaking. Everyone froze and none dared move a muscle.

"What's going on?" asked Arun looking a little scared.

"Tell him to shut up" screamed the masked man.

"Where is number 1?", he thought in his head, in their attempt to start the car, they had unexpectedly moved across the bend and it became easier for him to sneak up on them as he got plenty of cover but it also meant that his partner, who had them in his sights for a long time couldn't get a clear shot and had to relocate.

"What do you want?" Vivek inquired

"Right now, just do as I say."

"Coming in behind you, safe?" another voice was heard

"Safe" Another man dressed the same way appeared from behind the bend, holding a rifle pointed to the party in front of him.

He moved ahead and gestured to everyone to raise their hands"

"Raise your Hands Arun" Rohan said

"But why, what's happening?"

"Stop the engine!" Ordered the man with the rifle.

Tashi's legs were shaking by now. He went for the key, midway Shilpa held on to his shirt.

"Don't stop the engine" she whispered.

"Stop the engine and get out!"

"Drive! Drive! Get us out!" she whispered again without looking back, she had been seeing the whole thing through the other mirror.

The man with the rifle got closer as he passed Rohan and Arun and made them stand to one side.

"Drive! The engine is running, if you stop the car, it may not start again!"

"Hey! Stop the car and get out!" The masked man let out a warning shot and that was all that was needed, to plunge Tashi into action; he shifted into first and screeched off the road with Shilpa being flung back in her seat. The masked man looked at this and put his rifle to use, the rifle fired three round bursts, they all connected with the car, taking out the windows, puncturing the seats, hitting the panel. The music blasted out of the speakers as some wire had accidentally started the music system. The car hit the first set of the bad roads it had just overcome, Tashi was fleeing for his life, there was no question of taking it slow, he hit the card hard into the potholes and the entire car jumped on the road. Number 1 shifted from Semi to Auto on his rifle and let loose a barrage of gunfire aimed at the car. The random jumps the car was making going through the potholes didn't made the job easy for him, nor did the constant weaving that Tashi was doing. The roads were small but Tashi had been accustomed to driving in narrow mountain passes for years and pretty soon, the Car was out of the effective range of the of the Rifle and Number 1 watched hopelessly as the car kept getting smaller and smaller in his field of view. He brought his rifle down from his chin.

The masked man let of a slew of words in a language they didn't understand, came back angry and took it out on Rohan by plunging the butt of his rifle into his stomach. Riya shrieked seeing Rohan being pummelled but Arun was the worst affected, he didn't know what was happening and was by now, petrified. He simply waited and raised his hands up in the air as far as they went. In a brief moment, Riya, Vivek and Rohan saw each other and couldn't believe, that what remained perhaps the only way of them getting out of here was disappearing into the landscape and they are now, truly stranded, a feeling of complete hopelessness came over Rohan who felt he had been pushed to his absolute mental limit. He clenched his fists and silently cursed his luck for what was happening. Riya looked absolutely distraught as her mortality weighed over her. They were stuck, again.

27

Vivek and Arjun stood shocked in between the two masked Men.

The first one which had appeared still held on tightly to Riya's hair and showed no signs of relenting. "What do you know? Who are you?" they echoed the same questions and they gave the same answers.

"You, over there! Come here!" he looked at Arun's direction and ordered.

"He means you, idiot." Number 2 said as he looked to Arun.

Too frightened to move or say anything, Arun stayed in his position and didn't move, his hands raised straight and his face turned towards the ground.

"Get him here Number 1"

Number 1 grabbed him by the collar and made his way over to Number 2, stumbling.

Vivek cringed but did nothing. He wanted to say something but he couldn't. He was too scared to move or even say a word, whatever little bravery he had left, disappeared with the gunfire he had heard. The men had Arjun separated from them and warned him that any moment would mean their death. Number 2 let go of Riya's hair and she staggered as she held her hair nursing it. Number 1 flung Arun to the ground as he took a good look at the other people there. He walked over to Vivek who still had a cigarette burning between his fingers. He took it from him, drew in a long puff, exhaled and looked him square in the eye. Vivek looked away instantly and now looked towards the ground.

"Watch them" he said, Number 2 picked up Arun from the ground and looked at his face, smiled and moved a pistol in a circle in front of him.

"This one's blind as a bat!" he said in a way that made Vivek instantly look to him.

He let go of Arun and continued walking backwards, always making sure that he gave them no openings. It was what he was trained for. He kept a distance between himself and his team mate in a way that his line of fire never lined up with where the other was. He was trained, Arjun picked up on that, his small insight into Military practices told him that these men were trained, probably highly trained. The two came together, and with a gun still pointed to Riya's back. Number 2 dropped the cigarette to the ground and extinguished it. He signalled to Number 1, who spoke calmly and without a hint of emotion.

"I won't tell you who I am, I won't tell you where I am from and you will never be able to find out." Vivek was listening intently while Arjun was running his options in his head.

"This man, or rather what this man is in, is what we want."

"You are thieves then, is that what you are?" Arjun retorted

While number 2 moved ahead a bit, reacting to that name. Number 1 continued with the same expressionless manner.

"We don't care what you call us; we don't care if you think we are fairies. We want the suit, plain and simple, if you do that, we will let all of you go."

Arjun reasoned in his head, that there was no way that these people would let them live, he had killed one of their men, plus, there was no reason to let him live. Why would they suddenly be so generous? He looked over at Vivek who was silent for the longest time. He partly regretted having dragged them into this. It was no longer just his life that was on the line. Many ideas fluttered through his mind in what seemed to be a short time. Was it OK, to give this piece of technology to people that would possibly use it for dubious reasons? Was it OK to be trading off a country's secret? Were the lives of these people expendable in the long term? The thoughts didn't stop.

"We are prepared to demonstrate our resolve." he motioned to Number 2 who pressed the gun into Riya's back and smirked at them through his mask. Riya shivered nervously closing her eyes, tears clearly flowing down her cheek.

"No! No! Wait. Don't shoot, don't shoot!"

"Then give it to us."

"What I was thinking,"

"Number 2 Shoot." he said without even waiting for Arjun to finish his sentence.

"No Wait! I am coming out! I am coming out!"

Number 2 withdrew his gun from her back, but kept it pointed towards her. Just as Arjun thought, no openings.

"There is a protocol for coming out. I simply can't unbuckle! This isn't a roller coaster seat. "

"You will also show us the entry and exit protocols"

"OK, OK fine"

Arjun thought hard about his predicament and came up with no answer, maybe he could survive the bullets strapped in the ACE but the others won't. He finally said his first order set to come out

"ACE!"

28

"ACE!"

"Begin"…. His words were instantly interrupted by the volley of gunfire that rained around them. It cut them in two, Vivek, Arjun and Rohan on one side. Riya, Arun and 2 unknown's on the other. In the confusion, Vivek leapt at once on Number 2 and latched on to his utility belt, trying to overpower him during the confusion. However a man as trained as Number 2 could never be brought down by the likes of Vivek and his mad scramble. Vivek was quickly dealt with an elbow to his face and chop to his neck, He instinctively held his neck after getting hit with a blow but didn't let go of his hand on Number 2's belt, the belt broke off with it Vivek lost his footing and fell to the ground along with the broken belt. The firing intensified but didn't seem decisive; the firing seemed to be happening from far away. Arjun knew by know that bullets like pose a lesser chance to penetrate his heavy armour but still crossed his hands and covered his face while withstanding the barrage of gunfire. Rohan was still on the ground, too afraid to move, in this moment he thought that death had surely come for him. There seemed no escape this time.

 Both masked men dashed for cover.

"Who is firing at us?" Number 2 asked

"I don't know; right now let's get out of here."

"No! I won't chase it again! We are too exposed!

"What do you want to do?"

"Grab that woman!"

Number 2 grabbed Riya and placed a gun to her head, while Number 1 grabbed Arun by his hands and ordered him to get up. Both made their way behind the bend safe from the oncoming fire and began running while pushing both Riya and Arun to keep running.

"What's going through your head?" Number 1 asked.

"I'll explain, for now, just run".

Arjun, Vivek and Rohan lay exposed on the road. While Arjun was doing fine inside the suit, there was a very real risk to Rohan and Vivek. He move to the side of the valley, looked below and was just about to jump when the he looked back once again at the two cowering in the intermittent fire. He moved swiftly and covered Vivek and asked him to grab onto him. He did the same with Rohan, with his back towards the bullets, he rushed in the same direction of the masked men, the bend that they came over was the best chance at Cover. The came across, looked down and started sliding, he knew the ACE could take it. He had survived this far hadn't he? As they slid, Vivek looked helplessly as in the distance as the 2 men rushed off carrying Riya and Arun. The ice and small grains of rock irritated his eyes and face as they sled. The sliding continued for minutes as they finally managed to reach the base of the mountain. After coughing their lungs out Rohan and Vivek looked around and found them in the same situation that Arjun was in some time ago. They feared for their lives and dreaded what would happen next. Arjun had been through this experience and was reacting to it a little better than yesterday.

Rohan began silently crying as he felt the world spin and there was absolutely nothing he could do to stop this. The world he had lived in was drastically different; he was used to getting things done his way and never being pushed for anything. Arjun looked sympathetically towards them. He felt it was somehow his fault that these innocent people got involved. The two people from the group that the masked men let with were probably dead. Those bastards were using them as shields from the gunfire. He wondered if they would throw them off the cliff or simply shoot them both. One of those men seemed very cold and calculating, he was sure they would kill them. By now he was sure that they weren't Indian Army regulars, or Special Forces. Vivek held on to the Utility belt that had come off the masked man. He slung it across his shoulder.

"Keep moving for now, we can't stop, they can be upon us any time."

They walked on, with an uneasy pace, although Arjun wasn't running the large frame and height meant that for every one step he took they had to take two.

"What do we do now?" Rohan asked Vivek

"I don't know, I have been trying to figure it out. Who shot at us by the way?" Vivek enquired

"I think it was the Army" Arjun replied coldly

The reaction seemed to take both of them by surprise, they looked at each other, confused.

"Then who were those people around us? Were they not army?"

"No"

"Then who were they?" He said with a mixture of anger and frustration

"I don't know"

"That's not doing me any good! Why are people shooting at you man?" Rohan screamed as Vivek sought to restrain him, Rohan was losing his grip. They stopped as Vivek looked to calm Rohan down

"Hey! I just saved your life! If it was not for me, you would be filled with holes lying on that road!" show a little gratitude!

"Arjun, you need to tell us exactly what is happening here, no more lies, no more" Vivek said. "Everything is a mystery to us"

"Well, I guess we can stop for a moment" Arjun said as he viewed the sun disappear behind a mountain.

"I work for Accurate technologies, it's an engineering and software company, we specialise in operations that are not deemed fit for the rest of the tech companies to handle, I work in the liaison department of the company and was sent here as someone who could make a mock presentation for a product my company was trying to sell the Army"

"Yeah? You go around dressed like this?"

"This 'is' the product we were trying to sell"

They probably saw it coming once he told them that he was going to make a product presentation.

"Why is everyone shooting at you?"

"Things didn't go smoothly as planned, during the demonstration, the Suit misfired, killing 2 people, I tried to come out peacefully but they were too afraid of me." Arjun's voice dropped.

"I have been on the run since."

"Who were those 2 people then, Army?"

"I don't know about them, there was a third one as well, I was fighting him and from what I can piece together, during my fight with him, I fell of the edge of that mountain, The last thing I remember is falling, I must have hit my head hard against something, I don't remember much of that but that is when I must have collided with your car. The next thing I can remember is you trying to wake me up."

"Well, that explains a lot, what happened to the third man then, where is he?"

"I am quite sure he is dead. I shot him in the stomach." Arjun said this casually and without modulating his tone. "I am also sure, they were not with the Army" he continued. "Their clothes, their gear, their shoes were all wrong, it didn't seem like the kind of things an Indian Army personnel would wear."

"All this doesn't explain the gun fire we faced." Rohan interjected.

"My best guess is, it's the Army, they must have caught up to me and opened fire, they shot at me before too, It's also another reason I am sure that the masked people weren't from the Army, if they were, the Army wouldn't have fired unless they had a clean shot, why risk putting its own people in the line of fire? Also they could have just radioed them to stop, they did neither."

"What's going to happen with Riya and Arun? What about our friends?" Rohan continued.

"You ask me as if I know! I don't know! I don't know who they are; I don't know what's going to happen to your friends! In all likelihood, there are dead already. I saw them running with them and trying to cover their bodies, they were using them as shields, once they are out of range, they could have thrown them from the mountain or shot them! I don't know!"

"This is all your fault! All your fault!" Rohan screamed, "You first killed someone from the Army and after that you killed someone else!" "Now because of you, everyone is shooting at us. They don't care who we are!" "They want you!" "Because of you Riya is probably dead. The one person that I loved and for what?"

"Calm down Rohan! You are not helping!" Vivek said as he stood up

"Fuck you man! It was because of you that we are even here! You and your stupid Blind friend!

"Shut up Rohan."

"Oh you see Arun can't walk, hey Riya, hey Shilpa we have to take him in a car! I didn't ask for this! I could have walked to where we wanted to go; you and your charity case ruined it for me!"

"Shut up or I am going to punch you till you can't speak any more."

"Oh yeah! You are going to try too? You are going to kill me too?"

Rohan moved towards him and Vivek knocked him down, Rohan lay on the ground, crying his eyes out, Arjun couldn't bear to look at him, Vivek felt sorry for punching him but something had to be done. Rohan couldn't be left rambling. He instantly regretted what he had done, Rohan was not behaving rationally, he moved forward to console him, rant as he might have but he shouldn't have hit him. As he covered the steps, the radio on the utility belt chuckled to Life.

"Vivek".

29

"Base come in, this is Apollo"

"Go ahead Apollo"

"Patch me through to Hades."

"Hades here, go ahead"

"I don't know how to say this Sir, the plot seems to be thickening, the reconnaissance crew saw the targets surrounded by multiple persons."

There was a silence. Apollo went on.

"The recon crew were alerted by gunfire, they moved in closer of suspected point the point of origin, they found multiple targets standing close around the suit, and they took to firing"

"Why?"

"I don't know to be honest, they must have thought that they had the better position and tried to jump on them."

"What happened?"

"They miscalculated their distance, they were out of the effective range of their weapons, they appeared to have scattered them for now."

"Where are the troops now?"

"In pursuit, but they are being held back by the terrain".

"Hold them back, cancel the other combing troops, regroup and fan out from there."

"Right Sir."

"Apollo, we need to lock this up as quickly as we can, you are in interim command till then."

"Right Sir."

Brar looked around blankly staring at a picture of himself in full gear from around 20 years ago.

"Sir, we have your transport ready" the man said as he knocked on his door. He stood up, straightened his shirt, put on his beret and grabbed his suitcase and made way to the elevator waiting to take him to the surface. A Helicopter was ready to take off. Brar seated himself on the co-pilots seat, put on his headphones and the Bird lifted off. Leh Airport was prepped for soldier transport back to New Delhi. The Colonel got off the Helicopter and after signing off on a few documents seated himself on the place back to New Delhi. He looked outside the window, the snow covered Mountains of Ladakh seemed to glow Golden. In the setting Sun's light. He looked at the Soldiers who made their odd jokes about their wives and how they complained that their wives had threatened to leave them and go back to their mothers. The Soldiers kept to themselves and avoided interacting with the Colonel, except for a few smiles here and there. Enlisted men and Officers rarely mix.

There was a car parked outside the airport, it took him, the scene had changed so much, from the open wilderness of Ladakh to the now crowed Delhi Streets. The flight journey seemed shorter than the one on the road. He entered the military HQ with a specific purpose in mind.

The soldiers stood up and saluted him, as he walked through; he raised his right hand to his head, saluting them back. It was nowhere as rigid as the soldiers saluting him. He went for the most elusive room in the entire building. Project Trident...It was the command centre of the entire project. He negotiated the small hallways to reach central command. The nerve centre of the entire operation. A giant room appeared though a narrow door. The next in command greeted him with a salute. Brar got down direct to business.

"Get me in touch with Zeus and Poseidon"

"Yes sir" was the prompt reply.

Within Seconds, the giant screen in front of them read out the locations of both and communications link was established between all of them.

Two screens appeared on the screen in front of them, both relaying the co-ordinates of the two people he had asked for. Within a minute, Hades, Poseidon and Zeus were on the line. All threw took turns acknowledging each other's presence.

"Verify!"

The Colonel took out a small card which displayed random numbers, he fed the numbers into the number pad next to his seat. The Giant screen was still blank.

Hades Verified...

Zeus Verified...

Poseidon Verified...

Secure connection established. Establishing Visual Link

Two other Uniformed men appeared on the giant screen.

"Hades, we have received some disturbing news, it seems you have created some ruckus with your assigned suit man."

"Yes, he made a run for it, Apollo is currently in pursuit and we will find him before any more mischief can be attempted."

"Good to know"

"There is a specific reason I called this meet here." The Colonel took a pause"I hold the belief that a larger game in in play. We may be compromised to some extent. All my instincts tell me that the reach of any one of our enemies has been extended to this very operation."

"Impossible". Poseidon stated as if it was a matter of fact. This program is so far buried in paperwork and random funding siphons that no one could find it; they would, only if they knew where to look and what to look for.

"This is India." Zeus retorted, "A man's Conscience is sold cheap here. He may be right, for now, let's see what Hades is suggesting."

"Right, Gentlemen, I firmly believe that this fugitive wasn't working alone. My squad led by Apollo discovered that the accused is presently in the company of several people, none of them seem friendly to us, as was evidenced by 2 dead soldiers that perhaps the accused killed or the collaborators did it."

The expression on their faces went from disdain to complete attention. This was big news.

"Apollo is in pursuit and the matter of what the accused is doing in unclear, his movements seem to be quite erratic, it could be elaborate ruse to throw us off but I need to make sure that you are taking proper measures at your respective bases."

"Our operators did no such thing. Everything was under control here, I admit the sudden decision to go for an all-out demonstration did surprise me but knowing it came from you, I let it through."

"As a safety measure, I request you confine your operators to their quarters till this has been resolved, I personally don't think, we can use any more problems that we already have. Also for the time being, the suits need to be put under protection and watched 24 hours"

"I agree" Zeus replied almost instantly

"OK" Poseidon chimed in.

"Now, to another matter, to make sure the leak didn't happen from the Civilian side, We need to instantly investigate the background of the Accused, usual known acquaintances and most of all his company who was directly involved with the program. We need this done as stealthily and without raising any alarm bells. If the enemy currently believe that that our concentration is on the Man on the run, they must not realise that, the others are probably more at risk."

"Adding a little 2 cents, you were probably chosen given your relative isolation."

The colonel looked at Poseidon as he had said something unbelievingly stupid.

"You surely are on to talk about isolation, Poseidon."

"I am just saying, you were the closet to the borders and you were the target and that is the logical continuation of your theory that you have just presented"

"What aren't going to check with Accurate technologies? "Zeus asked breaking the silence.

"We are planning to get the NIA and the CBI on investigate"

"We have to go through the PMO."

"You are sure about this?"

"The only way to accurately track them is the NIA and CBI, The Army intelligence is no good there"

"Kronos won't be happy to hear that."

"Leave the situation to me; I know how to convince Kronos."

"We shall leave you to it then, in the meantime, I like your advice about keeping the operators restrained for now."

"Over and out."

Video link disengaged...

Brar got up from his seat to go see the man responsible for the operation. His head was filled with thoughts and how to present his Ideas to Kronos.

"Sir, there doesn't seem to be a connection at the HQ, he must have gone home." the telephone operator replied.

"Arrange a car and sent word that i would be coming in."

In around 20 minutes, the Car navigated the by lanes of Delhi Defence colony till it finally arrived at a bungalow. The bungalow had a very different vibe than the ones Military residences usually don't have this much artwork, sculptures lying in the lawn, visages of different Gods and goddesses at every corner and the quality of the garden suggested an experienced caretaker. The doorbell was rung and Brar waited outside. The almost never liked to wait for anyone. The Door opened and a Boy, who didn't even seem to be 18, opened the Door and inquired.

"Yes, May I help you"

"Yes, Son. Please fetch your father for me."

"Who may I say is calling?"

"Colonel Brar."

"Ok, take a seat Sir."

The colonel waiting in the living room of the spacious house. Lit by dim yellow lights, with Medals and trophies on one side and the adjoining wall adorned with photographs, each having its own light. The man came dressed plainly, the Colonel immediately stood up in attention and Saluted. The man saluted back with a weak effort and smiled at the behaviour. He gestured him to sit down, and went back inside after a few minutes, He came back in, opened a small wooden cupboard, Brought out a bottle of Whiskey and 2 glasses.

"I have asked the family not to bother us for some time." he said while seating himself in the chair opposite to Brar. He opened the bottle of whiskey and poured equal amounts of whiskey in both glasses. He gestured to Brar to lift up a glass while he held up his. Without a toast, both raised their glasses and had a small sip.

"I didn't know you were going to have a Chat with the others."

"I was necessary to have a chat with them to make sure that what was happening at my base wasn't repeating itself in the other locations . When the system was designed, it was designed so that the all three heads can only speak through a combined node access"

"Well right. What are you here to talk about, we spoke plenty today."

"It was something that we need to check Sir. I need your help to trace back the serpent back to its hole; I need your help in securing the locations and details of Arjun Joshi by putting the CBI and the NIA

163

on the case."

"That order can only come from the Prime minister's office, you understand that right?"

"Yes Sir, I am aware."

He got his phone out and called a number, he spoke briefly but simply asked the person on the other side to get back to him in 5 minutes once he disconnected the call, the man got up with the glass in his hand. He walked over to a wall where some pictures were hung. He examined the pictures closely, with such attention as if he was putting his eyes on them the first time.

"Sometimes, I think your moniker suits you more than your real name. You gave those Pakis hell that night."

Brar walked up to the wall and saw the photo, 11 people holding the Indian flag over a mountain top. Some bandaged, some talking the support of their fellow men, some standing strong.

"It's the only photograph of all you together."

Brar instantly looked down as a wave of nostalgia came rushing in. The looked into his glass while his mind replayed images of that night, the blood, the bodies, the bullets, the explosions. He remembered the heroism and the glory of his brothers in battle but most importantly he remembered how they were rewarded for it. He took another sip of that whiskey as the man watched whirling the whiskey in his glass.

"I never took it upon myself to ever ask you Brar, are you married?" the man said trying to ease some of the tension in the room

"No Sir."

"Ever?"

"Once."

"Children?"

"No Sir."

"I once thought that having children would be the end of me, you saw my son now didn't you?"

"Yes Sir."

"Growing into a fine man. He wants to be painter." he chuckled. "I wanted him to join the forces but sometimes he even accuses the Forces of being invaders and running the wheels of an empire". "He doesn't understand the work we do here, I doubt he ever will. Living in Delhi, attending college and dreams of painting. Trying to fight evil with his brush. If only he knew that evil can only be fought with evil. The good perish, the weak wilt away but the strong survive. No one, not even God can change that. The only good thing anybody can really wish for is a death without suffering."

"It does seem God has suffering in infinite supply, it's only the good things in life he seems to be limited with." Brar said looking at the photo and downing the rest of the whiskey in one go.

"Or is it the people above you who decide if you suffer, or you don't?" Brar asked vexedly

The phone rang, diffusing the situation. The Man picked up the phone after watching Brar coolly for about 2 rings.

"Right, the man in charge here is looking for Arjun Joshi. His Profile is, Executive at Accurate Technologies, presumed residence Bangalore. Current whereabouts, unknown. Make reports to my office, and be discreet about it."

"There, you have your request granted. "

"Thank you for the whiskey, Sir." Brar put down the glass on the table and presented a stiff salute, before moving around and starting to walk away.

"Brar, I think you never talk about that incident, you never have, it's the first time we are meeting at my home, have a seat, let's clear it out. Forget I am your CO for some time."

"I am sorry Sir; I have business to attend to." The Colonel said without turning around. "The only thing I can say is that perhaps your moniker suits you as well."

Colonel Brar marched out while he heard a woman's voice from inside reminded him that it was dinner time. He assured, that he would be joining them shortly, he walked over to the table, poured himself another peg of whiskey, sat down in the chair as he looked at the photo again he raised his glass to the photo and had sip. Brar exited the house a with a sense of having a wound reopened, he stopped ever so briefly when his car door opened stepped in and drove away from the house. The Name plate read, "Brigadier Prashant Bakshi".

30

Lying in the soft snow, Rohan was at the last straw of his nerves, it was everything he had hoped wouldn't happen. Arjun looked on, empathising with his predicament. Vivek was already in a bind, he wasn't behaving right as well, it wasn't normal for him to hit people. He moved over to help him when the Strap came to life.

"Vivek." said a voice buried in static and interference.

All three saw each other. Vivek looked at the strap and managed to pry open the compartment from which the sound was coming from,

"It's a Radio!" exclaimed Rohan.

"Thanks Captain Obvious!" Vivek's reply didn't seem to go well

"Open it!" ordered Arjun.

"I don't know how. How does this Work?"

"Vivek, can hear me?" the static sound and the interference was too much. The radio screeched and made weird noises but apart from random words, they weren't able to interpret anything.

"I can't make out the voice, it may be Riya!" Vivek gathered from those words and half-finished sentences. "We need to take this to a place where can get some range"

"It's probably because we are at the bottom of the mountain; we need to get to higher ground. There is a better chance of picking up a signal there" Arjun was right, there were at the absolute bottom, surrounded by more mountains on either side

"How? The climb is too great"

"We need not climb; we can simply walk in that direction. While we were falling, I thought I saw some open space there."

"Ok, let's do that"

Vivek took Rohan's arm, apologised profusely for laying a hand on him and backed it up by saying that different people reacted in different way due to the way they are. All three set out to the place that Arjun talked about earlier. Walking for a few minutes, Vivek asked Arjun, if it was a good idea to be exposed in an open area. Arjun explained that he would scout out the location first with the magnifier on board and make sure it was safe, before they would venture out. Vivek asked him if he could use the magnifier too. Arjun explained that the magnifier isn't an actual physical apparatus, the ACE is has some extremely high resolution cameras, they take a picture at very high resolution, probably over 100 mega pixels and simply zoom in to see a specific area or mark a specific region, The ACE had 6 cameras in all, 2 in the front, 2 in the back and 2 on both shoulders. Used simultaneously, they could generate a 360 degree rendition of the place around them. That data can be transmitted to mission control for analysis or other people who can watch his back for him, or so to speak. The Cameras in his back and on his left shoulder were damaged, he could only use his front facing and right shoulder camera but this was plenty. As they came across the open plain, they discovered that it was a lake bed with some water still in it, small glaciers opened up into the lake bed, the water looked in the process of freezing over, it had a very thin film of ice.

Rohan went to the waterfront and cupped some water in his hands after breaking the thin layer of ice. He spit it out instantly.

"The water is no good!" it's salty

"Brackish water" Vivek added, it can't be as bad as seawater but we shouldn't be drinking too much of it, it will kill us. Most of the lakes here have salty deposits.

"How did you survive without water? Rohan asked Arjun

"I didn't drink a lot of water; I ate the ice, little bits at a time. It was clean and I picked it, while some of it had frozen from rocks."

"Good idea, the ice will melt in the mouth or the stomach, so it's as good as having water."

"Also, not good, our bodies will start losing heat the most ice we eat, since it will go towards melting that ice. Haven't you seen those movies there the mountaineers get ice but then heat it over a gas stove so they can get liquid water?"

"Do you see any stoves Vivek?" Rohan asked condescendingly

"No, I don't." Vivek responded.

"Then it's our only option." Rohan went over to the small glacier, broke off a piece of ice and put it in his mouth.

The Radio started working again, this time the voice was loud and clear

"Vivek, Rohan can you hear me?" The message repeated itself 2 or three times in various tones. Both fumbled around with the small machine before they figured out that the round disc on the back has to be pressed in order to speak.

"We can hear you." Vivek said "It's good to hear your voice! Where are you?" Rohan put his hands up in the air and silently thanked god that Riya was alive.

"I don't know! These people are keeping us here"

Silence passed between them.

"Vivek, that's your name! Remember me?"

Everyone instantly recognised that voice; it was one of the masked men from before.

"Silent? No no, I can't have you silent."

"Where is Arun?"

"The blind bat was slow, we threw him off"

Vivek stood transfixed, frozen with terror, while Arjun and Rohan looked at each other.

"I am joking, he is here, alive!" Say hello blind Bat!" A slight moan was heard from the other side.

"Bastards! You let him go right now!" Vivek spoke with fury. Vivek was burning inside, the treatment of his best friend was driving him mad.

"Ok, should we throw him off or shoot him? We will do as you want." he added a chuckle to the end of the sentence.

"Let him go!" the voice intensified.

"What about your girl here? Can we keep her in exchange for the blind one? I wouldn't mind"

Vivek was seething with rage. The look on his face changed and even Arjun, looked slightly afraid to speak anything at this point. Rohan was happy to learn that Riya was alive but his face dropped when he realised that she is in custody. There was nothing they could do. Vivek held the radio, oblivious of what to do next. The last sentence burrowed into his heart. He was already murdering the man in his mind. He wanted to do that in real life too.

"Too much silence for too long. Did you leave?"

"What do you want?"

"Fair exchange, you bring in the suit guy and we will return these poor things to you."

"What?"

"Having hearing problems darling?"

"He is not with us any more, he took off when we touched the ground" Vivek looked over at Arjun as he lied through his teeth.

"1- Don't lie. 2- Don't lie. We know he is with you, where would he go?"

"I am not lying, he isn't with me, and he took off scared of you guys."

"Well then, that's too bad. I don't need these babies any more, Say your final goodbyes."

"Wait! Wait! I can find him"

"How will you find him? He has gone right?"

"I will find him!"

"Here is how it's going to work, you bring us the large metal man and take your girl away, and I am throwing the blind bat for free. How does that sound?"

"Why would he come?"

"Yeah, why would I go? Arjun asked between the exchange?

"I really don't care, I am on a schedule here, you bring me the man by the time I tell you and I will set the rest of you free. You have my word, no lies, and no games"

"Ok, Go on."

"Now, the question of how you will reach where I want you to come, you don't have a GPS on you do you?"

"I have one" Rohan said, excitedly, "In my phone; I have it in my phone."

"Yes, I have a GPS"

"Good now input these co-ordinates

34 degrees 55 minutes and 34 seconds North"

78 degrees 5 minutes and 3 seconds East"

I hope you have him here by tomorrow, if not, your friends die and we will have to come looking for you and give you horrible deaths too

Rohan noted the numbers as quickly as he could, he input the co-ordinates and soon a name flashed on the Screen.

.Kataklik Lungpa.

Rohan brought the phone towards Vivek, he looked at the phone and seemed confused, they both had never seen the name of the place, neither did they understand the route. The place seemed almost 50 kilometres away.

"Vivek, it doesn't show any roads"

"That is strange. Why are there no roads? Even the one we came by is not shown here."

Rohan made a face, which showed he had absolutely no idea.

"How long has it been since you updated this?"

"It's up to date, I updated it before I left Mumbai"

Arjun watched their conversation going back and forth and couldn't believe what was happening; they had already decided that he was going to go

"Wait a minute you morons, how have you decided that I am going to go?"

"Why of course you will! Riya and Arun are there in their custody" Rohan said

"That's bad for you but how does it affect me?"

"What are you talking about? Our friends are there because of you!"

"It was an accident, do you not see? And the way I see it, I saved your life too"

"You saved it, but it was endangered because of you"

"You have no idea what is going around here, you damned idiots, do you think that they are going to let your friends live? Do you think once they have the suit, they are going to let you live? You are nothing but idiots if you are so naive."

"So we let them die? So we let Riya die?" Rohan roared.

"I am sorry about your friends but I am not going anywhere, my life is just as important as theirs

Arjun stood up and Vivek knew there was nothing to stop him from staying, there was no motivation for him to go the place that the captors of his best friend and his love wanted him to come to. There was no way he was going to choose their life over his own. He didn't need to. He was right, he didn't know them and they weren't his friends. Rohan erupted in rage. He started going off on tangents that you couldn't threaten a man under these circumstances with. The

173

pointlessness of the whole ordeal vexed Vivek. He stood immersed in thought. Right now, everyone was the enemy. The two masked shooters were not the Army, Arjun had already established that. The Army was shooting at them, probably assigning guilt by association; they saw the group with the ACE and somehow postulated that they were in league with whatever Arjun was up to. He looked up and tried wondering why the helicopters weren't being sent in, to help with the search. There must be a reason. By this time a missing man such as Arjun would have caused quite a lot of panic everywhere. Maybe its national news and trending right now on twitter. Or maybe no one knows, after all this could be a major embarrassment to the establishment. In which case, the Government couldn't be trusted. Vivek walked up to Rohan who was still quite animated and trying to persuade Arjun into helping. Vivek asked for the phone from him. Rohan asked how could Vivek be was asking for the phone instead to trying to persuade Arjun. He didn't repeat himself. He took the phone and started at the screen. He took the phone away and sat on a boulder while running his hands on the screen. He studied it for a long time before shouting to the both of them.

"Hey!"

"I think there is a way we can all help each other."

31

"You think they will come?"

"Depends on how precious these people are" Number 1 replied still starting into the horizon

"I think the girl is to my taste." Number 2 said with a wicked smile

"Even if she is, you stay away from her"

"What's wrong in a little fun every now and then?"

"This isn't fun."

The two along with their captors were walking along with Riya holding on to Arun's hands. Except for the masked men, both were breathing heavily, they moved quickly out of the firing range and ran for quite some time, till Arun couldn't keep up any more. They weren't bound instead escorted by the two men, where would they run to? In the front were the mighty Himalayas and on their backs were these two men whom they couldn't overpower. They had nowhere to run. Their captors walked behind them with confidence, Arun held Riya's shoulder as she walked hesitantly across the frozen wasteland. They were walking around the bases of the mountains and not directly climbing them. It was still hard work and they hadn't experienced it in their lives. Riya grew tired of Arun's hand on her shoulder all the time, he was unconsciously also putting a little pressure on her, which resulted in her every step being a little heavier than the next. Riya stopped mid way and turned around.

"I need to go to the bathroom."

"So go." Number 1 replied.

"I need some privacy"

"You can't have it."

"I am a girl"

"I know" Number 2 said with a wicked smile.

"Please."

"It's the oldest trick in the book, they run a soon as they get the chance."

"I won't, Arun is still here"

"Hmm. Ok. Behind that boulder, go!"

The coast was clear, behind the boulder Riya saw the way to freedom, she went behind the boulder and stood there for some time. She thought about Arun and how she would be leaving him behind in order to escape. Once she started descended from that valley, there was no way that they could catch up to her. Her mind went to Arun again, would it be ok, if she just left him there. Would it really be that bad? Arun was a blind man, if she even tried to help him escape, the problem of holding his hand or guiding him for the entire way seemed idiotic. She would never have made it out in time. She thought quickly about abandoning Arun to his fate. If someone was making it alive out of this situation it was her. Arun could not be saved.

In the meanwhile, Number 2 was close to Arun when he spoke

"Does it feel nice to imprison a blind man?"

"I don't know, i have never done it before? When I am through with it, I shall tell you."

"Have some fear of God, He won't let you go easy"

"Sure."

"My whole life was spent being the person who didn't get anything, my whole life was spent in obsessing over how sight would be" He had both of their complete attention.

"So how would sight be, how would you understand about a different sense if you have never experienced it?"

"Don't talk number 2"

"I don't know" replied Arun. I have no idea.

"Blind as a bat, just as I suspected."

"You are going to kill us aren't you" Arun asked getting a little emotional

"No, No, Whatever gave you that idea? We said maybe we will kill you maybe we will spare you"

"Please don't kill me, Please don't" Arun said as he fell to his Knees.

Number 2 laughed and looked at Number 1. Number 1 wasn't overtly shocked by this behaviour, the human tendency to survive is uncannily strong, and there knelt a man before them that had no power whatsoever over them. Number 2's sadistic tendencies began to surface.

"Tell me a joke."

"A joke?"

"Yes, a Joke."

"Please, I don't know any joke"

"No, I will tell you one, I once killed a man! Get it?" The man laughed wildly, Number 1 was still not amused. He instantly stopped laughing and looked at Arun, he took a step closer.

"Ok, there were 2 tigers"

"No forget it, sing a song, I have changed my mind"

"Which one?"

"Any one, wait you know what, what songs are taught to small children? Those nursery rhymes, Go on do it!" He said with a jovial tone, he studied his face and got even closer, He got to his ear and whispered, "Do it"

"Uh.. Twinkle Twinkle"

"Nope, stop. Dance for me. If you dance for me, I will be happy." he said walking backwards a few steps.

Number 2 started humming a tune and Arun stood frozen, too embarrassed to react, Number 2 came closer singing some traditional songs. Eventually coming across and scaring Arun by touching the muzzle of gun to his arm and prodding him to move. Number 1 watched all this and didn't move a muscle. He wasn't going to interfere. But he hated it and was beginning to detest this spectacle. Arun started jumping and making some movements that he could manage. Number 2 egged him-on to jump higher and higher. Number 1 would often baby talk and repeat the word 'not enough'. They tried doing that till Arun had no life left in him. Arun slid and collapsed to the ground, crying. Number 2 coldly returned to his position and didn't utter a word except smiling to Number 1. Arun still on the ground begged again for them to let him go.

"You don't need me! You need the girl!" Arun cried.

Number 2's interest piqued. He came back out again and bent down to Arun's level

"Explain"

"Both of those guys behind me have a crush on her."

"Wow! Love! We haven't seen it in a long time, have we number 1?"

"If you let me go, they will still come, they will still try to free her, you can just let me go at a village or even if you let me go here, someone will come for me." Arun said, holding back tears

"Tell me more about this love thing, I want to know" Number 2 asked excitedly

"Riya, that's her name. She was the one who planned this trip; it wasn't me or anyone else. She planned it and brought us here. The ones there are Rohan and Vivek. They are in love with her and will go to any extent to get her back"

"What an amazing story, love stories are so heart-warming; I am going to remember that one for tomorrow"

"I have told you everything, please."

"Ok, last thing and I will let you go. Walk and bark like a Dog"

Arun felt another rush of tears welling to his eyes. He had never been this humiliated throughout his life. Reluctantly after a lot of prodding by Number 2, he got on all fours and started walking in the snow covered path.

"Hey, Bark!" Number 2 Screamed angrily

Continuously fighting back tears and with a low voice, Arun reproduced those sounds but finally wept.".

"Please, Please let me go"

"Dogs like you can't be let loose, you can either be tied to a post or put down in the street. We were never going to let you go. I lied!"

Arun started bawling and Number 2 pointed at Arun and said,

"Pathetic."

Riya was trying to make her escape and unfortunately she found out, that what seemed like a straightforward route from just 50 meters back turned into a dangerous incline and what seemed to be a deadly drop. She cursed her luck for bringing her here and made the difficult but safer decision to turn back and remain in custody. As she made her way back, she heard voices of distress, He made it closer to find Arun crying on the ground as Number 2 watched and smiled. Number 1 remained stoic; he neither encouraged nor discouraged his comrade. A twitch of anger passed through her, more so because of number 2 and not because of what Arun was doing.

"Ah! You are back. You just missed it! He was doing a very good Dog impression"

Riya went forth and lifted Arun up and simply asked the masked men to keep moving. She wasn't going to engage in pointless debates that did not end well for anyone. She would shout, they would prolong the discussion and ultimately, since right now, they have the power. Arun and she would have to ultimately bow down to their way. Any words would be wasted on them and he had potential of increasing their suffering but mostly she was disappointed that she could not get away, she couldn't run away. Second thoughts popped in her mind, should she have jumped? Was it worth the risk? She thought about it repeatedly and couldn't make up her mind. She was stuck here and that's all there was to it.

As the 2 captives moved ahead in the evening sun, the Captors engaged in some conversations of their own.

Number 2 remarked to number 1 about the her behaviour,

"Did she seem angry to you?"

"Yes."

"Don't you think it at least a little bit sexy?"

"No"

"Come on, how long as it been? We are going to kill them anyway."

"Number 2, watch what you speak."

"You are being too serious now, you can partake too. The secret is buried between the two of us."

"Number 2," he said, as the 2 captives went a little far ahead, "I have had enough of this distasteful behaviour" He said as slowly as possible but he made sure his eyes relayed the message loud and clear.

"Your behaviour back there does not resonate with the high standards, the traditions or the principles of our party or our Army. What you did there was horrible. There was no reason to treat a civilian that way"

Number 2's face suddenly had the look of seriousness as he replied

"So, what should I have done? Give them a reading of the Geneva Convention? War, we are at War. Isn't that what were told before we were sent here? Isn't this what we do?

"A good soldier thinks not only of the loss of life of his comrades but also the life of the enemy's. If a life isn't required to be extinguished, then there is no need to go through with it.

"Idealist" he said as he laughed for a few seconds, his face went serious again as he asked him a question. "We are going to kill them right? There is no point in thinking what would traumatise them, the biggest trauma of their lives lies in front of them. They are ours, our prey. I like to play with mine. I am going to kill them but slowly, and I will enjoy it. You see what I am wondering is, if someone is going to die, why would I bother with the type of death I give them?"

"Because there is no point of their suffering."

"Tell me, do you believe in a God?"

"What does that matter? What is the point of that question?"

"Oh but there is, tell me. Do you?"

"Yes."

"God writes the destiny of everybody, the small and the large, the black and the white, the old and the young along with the Able bodied and the disabled, if you believe in God, you must also believe that the decision of whether or not I kill this man or let him go is already made by him a long time before any of us met or were even born. The strings of destiny move our hands; we are mere puppets to it. If it is that man's destiny to die by my hand, he will. His entire life has been moving towards the moment of his death. The moment he was born, it was decided that he would die by a bullet to the dead by me or by falling down from a mountain. There are no two ways about it. He can't change what is going to come. Hell! Even I can't change what is going to come and I am not even sure how I am going to kill him, but the decision has been made. You see, I am no more guilty of killing him as much as God is. God led them to me; I am the instrument of God's will. Out here, I am the hand of God. The one with power in his hands."

"Such thinking is not allowed within the party!" Number 1 furiously replied.

"We are a long way away from home, jurisdiction doesn't apply". Number 2 said coldly. "Imagine If I were to harass this blind man and eventually kill him, then have my way with that girl and then kill her too, wouldn't that be their destiny? Why should I be punished for what happened to them? You see number 1, if you believe there is a God; you must accept the outcome of that belief.

"You are going mad, when did you come up with this?

"Being alone in the snow gives you a lot of time to think about the man upstairs, it makes you realise how his head works and more importantly what he wants. The inevitable outcome of a belief in God is simple, there is no free will. No free will for you nor for me. As I said, we are puppets held together by the strings of destiny. He weaves the string, and makes the invisible string dance in the darkness of the cosmos. Without his will, a leaf cannot fall from the tree. Do you really think that men who get murdered, women who get raped, children that are abused by their parents are really the result of other people?

"It's the people, they have a choice, and they have the free will of weather choosing a good path or a bad path. That will lead them to their ultimate justice"

"It is the illusion of choice Number 1, not choice itself and certainly not free will."

"You are making no sense; there are good people and bad people in this world"

"There are no good people or bad people. The people have no choice; they can't inherently be good or bad. If what you say is true, then it's the free will of the Murderer to kill or rapist to rape but what about the free will of the man who doesn't want to die or the woman who doesn't want to be raped? Even still, you can't think of the suffering of the parents of a child who has bone cancer and will die in a few years in a horrifying way. What about the free will of the child who doesn't want the cancer running amok in his body or is too small to comprehend what was happening to him?

"He moves everything. Every piece on the board game of life. That is why I find these trials for heinous crimes funny. I think in my head, if God approved that act and if his justice is absolute, who are you to try these humans? Even Hitler, who was responsible for the genocide of 6 million Jews, died a coward's death by ingesting poison and shooting himself. How was that justice to the millions he arranged to be killed like animals? How was that justice to them? There is a famous story about a few words etched into one the concentration camp walls that a victim wrote, he said, if there is a God, he will have to beg for my forgiveness. Even he didn't get it. Why would God give a damn about your forgiveness?

Number 1 took a good look at Number 2, he was walking slightly ahead while letting out a loud laugh after completing his sentence. He was clearly going mad. He knew that Number 2 was a little unhinged but this conversation proved that in all likelihood, even if he didn't display the insanity more often, or in front of others, he was no longer fit to serve any more. There was no telling what he would do. He had to be on guard from him as well.

32

"What have you figured out?" Arjun enquired

"Look at this Map, it's around 50 Kilometres away right?"

"Yeah so?" Rohan chimed it.

"Look at the area. It's some place called 'Kataklik Lungpa', now I don't know what it is, but look, it's so close to the border with C.O.K"

"What's C.O.K"? Rohan asked.

"C.O.K is Chinese occupied Kashmir, or Rather the Aksai Chin Area. The Indians and the Chinese went to war over it, way back in '62. Just like P.O.K, the current status quo hasn't changed. They maintain control over the other side of the border, and we maintain control here"

"So what about it?"

"I am now convinced that whoever these people are, must need a way out, their only choice is to get you or the suit into C.O.K, that's their safest bet to be secure but at the same time its also a pretty dumb idea."

"Why is that?"

"Because of the Line of Actual Control is very close to it, there is a possibility of a lot of troops in that region maybe a lot of forward operating bases or even bunkers set up to monitor activity. The Chinese have been very aggressive in the last years, so there remains a chance that they could be around, patrolling or monitoring just to keep an eye on the Chinese"

"Isn't that bad for us though?" Rohan asked

"Not necessarily, you see, until now, we haven't really encountered a lot of Army forces, in fact none that confronted us directly, only Arjun has directly encountered fire. If the news really would have gotten out, they would have been using Helicopters and Satellites to track us right now. That isn't happening or at least isn't happening uptil now. This leads me to believe that I am correct in assuming that this event is an isolated one, and no one, not even the Army wants to fan its flames. Lest it become too big a fire to attract attention. Isn't that right?"

"To be honest, my project was quite secretive, not many know about it, even those who did know, knew in parts. The officers didn't see the suit before yesterday and even I wasn't briefed about it till 4 weeks ago, it is unlikely that the existence of the ACE would be common knowledge within the normal ranks."

"What's ACE?"

"It's the name of the suit, the Advanced Combat Enhancer"

"That's such a stupid name." Rohan chuckled.

"Why is that? It's a brilliant name."

"It does seem unimaginative." added Vivek.

"Hey, let's get back to the plan here."

"Yeah sure, sure. What I was thinking of is really quite simple, If were to travel to this location, and I don't know how we are going to do that but if we are, then we could do one of two things or both. The People, who were looking for Arjun and now unfortunately us, will follow our trail, currently it's safe to say that they are behind us and not doing a great job catching up to us. But we can motivate them to try and catch up just a bit, or alert them that we would be travelling to Kataklik Lungpa, then they would make sure that they reach there before we do, maybe even intercept us midway. There they would be hard pressed to carry out any kind of stringent or over the top manoeuvre because of the presence of other troops in the vicinity. If we remain here, there is a possibility that they could launch a heavy attack because this is a wasteland with no one here. If we are able to somehow talk to them. We could delay the masked men long enough for them to lay an ambush and kill these other two masked people. We would have surprise on your side, right now those two think that the army group hunting Arjun is also hunting us, since they can't differentiate between the two. They would have no way of knowing we spoke to the army fellows We can then get our friends back and you can explain yourself to them without having them fire bullets at you.

"What's the other plan" Arjun asked.

"We get there, get these guys there too, start firing and have the regular army as well the ones behind us engage in an all-out battle with the Masked men, therein lies the risk, if they are still using Arun and Riya as shields their life would be put in grave danger, more than what it is right now."

"Umm. Yeah, how about no!" Rohan replied

"The first one carries more merit"

"No it doesn't" Rohan said, "If the Army guys following us want the exact same thing that the masked men want, what's to stop them from telling you to give them the suit first and killing Arjun and us on the spot?"

"We don't know that for sure and even if they do, we simply tell them that they would get the suit once we are done with getting our friends back."

"That doesn't clear anything up" Rohan said slapping his forehead and pacing up and down animatedly.

"The only way it could work is if they knew for sure that we are not screwing around with them and they have a method to trust us. They would need a gage of some kind, some kind of security or guarantee, to show them that we aren't lying" Arjun said

Vivek nodded in agreement. For this to work, they definitely needed something, or even if nothing, they needed a bargaining chip, the Chip was the ACE, and everyone seemed after it. Till they had the ACE, they held a slight advantage. Vivek carefully analysed the situation

"There is also, another major problem that we haven't to be talked about."

Vivek looked up to Arjun from his pensive stance, he wasn't expecting another obstacle.

"The suit isn't fully configured yet, so the suit and the batteries aren't calibrated together to handle the extreme levels of stress that the suit is facing. The batteries are currently down to 38% and by this time tomorrow, they could very well be completely gone. If I keep using the suit, the batteries will drain faster and to survive the night outside, we will have to use the heat function. There is an emergency 10% reserve but I am not sure that the suit was programmed with it and since I don't have a compatible system to check it, there is no way to know for sure. Maybe it has it, maybe it doesn't. We shall come to know tomorrow, when the batteries touch 0."

This complicated things, this also put a time limit to the window they could get the suit delivered in time, Vivek had no intention of handing the suit over to the masked men but considered that option in the face of losing Riya and Arun. He also considered the option that they would kill both of them regardless of him delivering on his promise. If the suit doesn't last out the night, then there was no use of planning the elaborate flow of the events for tomorrow. The army would catch up to them and that would be the end of it. They would never see Riya or Arun. Most likely, Rohan and he would have been thrown in Jail for a charge that either wouldn't exist or since they were so far off, they could be imprisoned indefinitely or bumped off in the worst circumstance. His mind went to Tashi and Shilpa who had taken off.

"There is more." Arjun interjected his train of thought.

"Please, no more" Rohan said

"I can cover the 50 Km's I have read that in the manual, it shouldn't be a problem but I doubt I can do it with two of you holding on, or even one of you."

"You are a huge machine, it shouldn't be a problem for you." Rohan said.

"Think about it." Arjun added, "Both of you must weigh around 80 kilos, that means an additional 160 kg's that this machine wasn't rated to handle. Even if it could take the load, which I don't doubt. That means more work for the motors of the machine and more work means more energy spent. Which ultimately means faster battery drainage. So while I think one of you, could somehow make it with me for 5o Km's, the possibility of both of coming for the ride you is simply not possible"

Rohan, at this point started laughing and both Vivek and Arjun turned at him to check the possibility that he was going mad. It was simply a laugh of desperation mixed with frustration. The odds were overwhelming and no clear route seemed in sight. They had to get their friends back in a way that meant keeping themselves alive while being hunted one side by the Indian Army and on the other side by skilled people of dubious origin. Rohan's continuous laugh started making Arjun uncomfortable but he knew from what he saw a few minutes back that he was having a really bad day and let it slide, while giving Vivek a slight visual cue. Rohan stopped laughing looking at the lake and coughed while he turned around and asked Vivek the only question that mattered.

"Who is going to stay?"

"I don't know Rohan."

"You really were bad news you know that?"

Vivek simply looked away while making a frown

"Ever since you have come, there is this huge wedge between Riya and me."

"There is no wedge between Riya and you."

"Oh yeah, there is, it's you."

"And how is that?"

"Ever since you came in her life, it's been this way. I am better looking, I have more money and I have things I can give her. I have the better life. What do you have?"

"Am I supposed to answer with "I have my mother?"

Arjun snorted listening to that. Only to get an angry glare from Rohan.

"This was supposed to be our trip, Shilpa, me and Riya, you even brought her to your side."

"Dude! What are you talking about? She was on nobody's side! She escaped as quickly as she could remember?"

"You used her to make Riya feel differently about me."

"Look, I don't know why she hasn't told you this before, or maybe she has but you are too thick headed to listen to it. Riya and you don't click. You just don't. It's been 12 years since college; you need to let it go. Riya didn't like you then, she doesn't like you now. You are a friend to her simply because you kept in touch, nothing else. You were in touch with Shilpa just because you were in touch with Riya! I have been there dude! I know what it's like not to be liked or loved. I know this isn't going to be easy to do you have to start to learn to let go man, or it's going to keep haunting you your entire life."

"I am not letting anything go."

"Fine! But in the meantime, if you want to save the girl you love or claim to love, we are going to have to work together and save her. Or is that concept too hard for you to understand? Or do you need to go into another one of your crazy man speeches?"

"You don't get to decide who gets left behind."

"We will let luck decide, bring out a coin and let's toss for it then. Vivek responded while he angrily got of the rock he was sitting on.

Rohan opened up his purse and got a coin out, he threw it in the air and Vivek called heads. The coin landed on heads. Looking at his expression, he asked him to a best of three, Rohan tossed the coin again and it landed on tails. A smiling Rohan flipped the coin again and this time, it landed on heads. Vivek looked at Rohan again and asked him for a best of 5. Arjun looked that this game over a girl and started reminiscing. The coin toss reminded him of something he kept fondly near his heart. The game of luck landed once in favour of Arjun and the last toss saw it decisively land in the favour of

Vivek. He had given him 3 chances. He now looked at Rohan's face, the same look of dejection loomed.

"Any more?" Vivek asked loudly raising both his arms to the side with palms outstretched

"Fuck off man!"

Vivek walked back to Arjun and asked him his opinion about how they could get the army guys to chase them.

"It's pretty straightforward; someone from among us would have to initiate contact"

"They would have to be risk getting shot?"

"From what I gathered in the small time I have been with you, you seem to be a smart guy, so figure it out.."

"Well, Damn."

"What about the radio?" Arjun asked, can't we just radio the army guys?

Vivek checked the radio and fiddled with it. "It doesn't broadcast on any other frequency. It's locked to the frequency that the two men have. So we can't radio anyone else. It would have been better that way but it isn't. Also getting the jump on them is impossible, even normally trained army guys are better aware of their surroundings than the civilians."

"Wait for them to come to you, show them you mean no harm, and quietly go further"

"How long do you think it would take for them to reach our location?"

"Three, maybe four hours down the mountain then another hour or two to get to this place. Maybe, I can't be sure"

"That gives us plenty of time"

"It would also be pretty dark by that time."

"How do we make Rohan appear non-threatening?"

Rohan went off to the side to relieve himself, while Vivek looked around at the rocks and let out a smile, he told Arjun his plan which caused him to break out into laughter.

"What's so funny?" Rohan quipped, zipping his pants"

"Rohan, this is going to sound a little strange, but trust me, it's all going to make sense in the end"

33

The Meeting with Kronos left Brar with a bad taste in his mouth, he thought back to those wretched memories that Bakshi had managed to bring back to the surface. The car brought him to his official residence. He would fly out to Leh again tomorrow. It was too late in the night to fly sorties and it would arouse unnecessary suspicion in the community. His thoughts remained with his soldiers. He was in every sense a dedicated commander, thinking primarily of the life of his men and their comforts, even the ones he didn't like. The Army was his life. It was all he knew. He sometimes wondered about what he would do once he was out of the Army. He had his mind set on dying before that happened. The Colonel looked at his doorman and asked him to arrange something for dinner. The man rushed outside leaving another guard in his presence. The colonel unlocked his door and entered his empty house. Everything looked as if it had stopped. The pas came rushing back ."I hate Delhi." He exclaimed to himself.

He thought of his parents and his wife, the ones who lived here before, in this now empty, soulless place. After the war, and his actions in it, he would never have to set place on the front-line ever again. Strangely, it was the only place he wanted to be after that night. The idiosyncrasies of normal life seemed too much to bear. The family life and the constant need for mediocrity from the ones closest to him seemed to arouse in him thoughts of disgust and disbelief. He loved them but never understood how they could place a life over an idea. The only thing they exuded was their selfishness. That became the distance between them. The Parents left to live with another brother and now were both dead. His wife gave him an ultimatum of quitting the service or staying married. Brar chose the former. They didn't understand. They never understood. Only the services understood. He thought of marrying again, to someone more understanding. He wasn't a young Captain any more. The years had taken their toll on his face. The constant exposure to harsh climate, the heavy drinking, the disregard for anything that seemed weak. It wasn't going to happen. The World had changed but for Brar, it had remained the same. The same place, same problems, just newer people. The phone buzzed, it was someone from Bakshi's department. Someone from the CBI had started the trace for Arjun Joshi. He kept his phone away, and undressed to settle in. There was a time when scars on his back and leg made the people shout "Hero!" Now they just move on slightly disturbed by the sight. The heroes of yesterday are the fools of the present.

The Phone buzzed again, as the Colonel now sat down for dinner and was about to put the first morsel of food in his mouth.

"Yes."

"Sir, Priority one."

"Can it wait?" Brar asked looking at the morsel of food in his hand

"No Sir,"

"Patch him through and make sure its most secure line possible."

"Hades?"

"Yes Apollo, Go ahead"

"Sir, we are not quite sure how to describe this."

"What is it? Speak up man!"

"Sir, we started the combing operation again after regrouping. We wanted to do our best to find out where the ACE went, in the search we came across a lake bed a few hours from the initial place of sighting."

"Ok," The colonel said, impatient with the morsel still in his hand.

"Well Sir, We have found a man under, strange circumstances"

"What strange circumstances?"

"Sir, it seems this man was bound, and left here"

"By Whom?"

"We have no idea, Sir."

"Who is it? Who is the man?"

"We haven't freed him yet; I thought it would be better to ask you first, this didn't seem like normal situation. He has been mumbling a lot but his voice isn't clear through the handkerchief that's gagging his mouth."

"Well open him up."

Rohan's hands had been bound by his own scarf while his legs were bound by Vivek's. He was left standing and around him, up to his chest, Arjun had arranged rocks in a circle close to his body. Rocks heavy enough that he couldn't dislocate them without the use of his arms and legs. Neither was there enough space for him to bend his legs. , he was finally gagged by his own handkerchief and was trying to scream for a long time. Apollo instructed the Jawans to remove the handkerchief from his mouth. Rohan coughed and instantly asked for water.

"Those Sons of Bitches did this to me! Let me out! Let me out!"

"Language." Apollo scowled

"Get me out of here please!"

"First, who are you and for what are you doing here in the middle of nowhere?"

Colonel Brar also listened through the line

"My name is Rohan Dalal. I am from Mumbai, I am tourist"

"There are no tourists allowed in this region"

"Well, I didn't know that! Tashi didn't say that"

"Who is Tashi?"

"My driver"

"Where is he?"

"How am I supposed to know?" Rohan said

"Why did he leave you here like this?"

"No he didn't leave me, that bastard Vivek did!"

"Son, you are taking names I don't know off, you better start making sense real soon."

"Ok, I will tell you everything but can you take me out first? Please! I beg you! I have been standing for 4 hours, I want to sit down."

"Sir?" Apollo inquired.

"Your discretion Apollo"

"Jawans, bring him out of there and untie him"

The Jawans moved the heavy rocks aside and as they fell, it was revealed that Rohan was bound hand and leg. Once the Soldiers finished moving the rocks they first patted him down and after making sure he didn't have weapons on him, they opened his binds.

Rohan staggered and sat on the ground with a thud. He massaged his wrists and Legs while muttering expletives. He asked for water from one of the Jawans and he handed him his canteen. After taking a large mouthful, He almost choked on the water. He felt nauseous and rudely rebuked the Jawan for carrying such bad tasting water. Apollo watched the entire episode with part suspicion and part humour. He walked up to him and asked him to tell the full story.

"As I said, my name is Rohan Dalal, I am from Mumbai, I am a tourist and our Driver Tashi took us on a tour promising to show us snow leopards, it was Tashi, me and 4 other people in the car. While we were on our way on a mountain pass, something collided us." Rohan continued, "We didn't figure out what it was. It just seemed like a large metal object with a man inside it. It was unconscious when we found it."

"Joshi!" remarked the Colonel.

"Yes that's what he told his name was, Arjun Joshi."

"He collided with us and damaged out car. While we were trying to start the car, he awoke and while we were scared of him, he somehow helped get the car running again by pushing the car."

He held the complete attention of all the Jawans, Apollo and Brar. This was a story no one had expected..

"While we were just about to get in and drive away, 2 masked men came up from behind the bend and took everyone by surprise, they wanted what Joshi was wearing. They had rifles and were covered from head to toe, we couldn't see their faces, and they had some kind of gear with them. All of that seemed advanced and professional they wanted the suit. They asked him several times to remove it and give it to them. Tashi and Shilpa somehow escaped as they were both in the car but the rest of us got trapped in this mess. They pressed him again for the suit and they were threatening to kill Riya if Arjun didn't comply. Just when he was about to do that, Bullets started hitting the area and everything went chaotic.

"Sir, I think, this is where the Recon group fired"

"Yes, that seems right"

"The firing broke the group into two and the masked men, finally took 2 of our friends hostage Riya Mehta and Arun, I don't remember his last name but he is blind"

"Go on,"

"Arjun grabbed on to us and Slid down the valley and when we started picking up some radio signals"

"How did you get a radio?"

"Vivek had held on to one of the masked men and his best came off, The belt was in his hands as we fell, to get better reception, we walked here, hoping that the reception would be better." Rohan's face now dropped. "We did get a message, the other 2 men now have our friends in their grip and they are holding them hostage. We don't know where they are but what we do know is that they want the suit and they gave a place to us that they wanted it delivered to. If if don't do that, they will kill both of them. Sir, Please save them"

"Which place was this?"

"some katalik lunga something, I am not sure"

"Kataklik Lungpa?" a Jawan suggested

"Yes, that's the one".

"That's all fine but why did they leave you here in this way?" Apollo asked still a little puzzled by the circumstance of his discovery.

"They thought it would be good idea to warn the people pursuing us that we were not the enemy and that they thought, if you could set up an ambush beforehand, we would be able to kill the masked men as well as recover our friends and save them from harm. Till that Bastard Vivek had this stupid idea to bind me, cover me in stones and gag me with the help of that giant metal freak. "Apollo couldn't help but force a smile as he looked at Rohan with the radio still in his hands. Brar too was slightly amused.

Vivek's gamble had paid off. He based his idea on the belief that the Army wasn't out for blood, they were simply trying to chase down a rogue element. Given the circumstances of the day, it was bound that all of them would have itchy trigger fingers; they could have shot him if they thought he could move or considered him dangerous. Given the alternative of encountering a man who was bound and gagged they would have let down their guard and tried to proceed without the feeling of Danger. At least that was the idea, it had worked, the people around Rohan were now relaxed and not raising their guns to take aim at him.

"Your friend, Vivek, you said. Did this?"

"Yes, that Asshole, if I ever see him again, I am going to beat the hell out of him."

Apollo let out a laugh, so did some of the other Jawans. Rohan looked dumbfounded

"Your friend is a smart man." Apollo remarked. As Rohan still continued look confused as to what happened around him.

"Sir, what happens now?"```

Brar pushed his leg back a bit under his chair and thought hard, The Location of the rendezvous point was close of the Line of Actual Control, it was a sensitive zone and these masked men were a new addition to the story. He thought of the message that was conveyed, it was clear that the men who had popped up were after the suit. Why and what their endgame was, was still a mystery. There wasn't a clear idea of what would happen if Apollo and his group went forward with the plan that was just suggested. At this point it could just be another trap and it could lead to more deaths.

"Could it be Pakistanis Sir?" Apollo asked

"No, not a chance. Not on this side of the border, plus they were too well equipped from what this fellow says, their infiltration parties usually consist of small arms and poor protection gear "

"Mercenaries?"

"I am not sure. There hasn't been that kind of activity in this part of the world, there isn't much that the mercenaries would be paid for. They would have to be intelligence agents, if I have to bet"

"Hey, Rohan"

"Yes Sir, Were they speaking any language you understand?"

"They had a very thick accent when they spoke, and while they did speak privately it wasn't Ladakhi or Kashmiri, I have heard that Language"

"So foreigners for sure."

"Yes, although their faces were covered, so I didn't catch a look at their features"

"Sir, guess we will have to hunt them down then." Apollo spoke with confidence

"Looks like that" Brar beamed with confidence. He felt his faith in Apollo renewed, he didn't make a mistake with him. He was the right person for the job.

"Sir, wouldn't it be easier if we followed the present course of action and went to Kataklik Lungpa and laid a trap for these people"

"It would seem so, I leave it to your discretion, brief me once you have a plan of action and I will join you tomorrow.

"Right Sir, over and out".

Brar kept his phone down and remembered the morsel of food in his hand, the food on the plate also was cold now. He sighed and bit into the morsel and then ate the rest of his meal without a word or thought. Tomorrow was a big day.

34

The valleys and the landscape whizzed about as Vivek hung on to Arjun as he made quick work of the distance. The wind unforgiving and Vivek put his head down to avoid the wind hitting his face. They had been going for hours and by now Vivek was completely exhausted. He spotted a few trees from the corner of his eyes. He hit the top of suit 2 times and pointed in that direction. Arjun quickly changed course and went to the tree line. After reaching the spot, Vivek tried to get off with care but fell off the suit, his legs were numb and so were his hands, they didn't have a lot of movement in them. Arjun helped him to sit up while Vivek asked him how many more Kilometres to the exchange area. Arjun checked his HUD and mentioned that it was only 7 more kilometres to the area. Vivek reconfirmed it by checking the GPS on Rohan's phone while his hands shook, Vivek looked in bad shape The tress were against the side of a mountain which looked as if there was a cave in its side. Arjun helped Vivek to his feet and slowly guided him towards the cave. Arjun looked around and using his strength broke down the branches of some of those trees and then broke them into small pieces. His HUD flashed.

Charge level 15%

He immediately started the exit protocol and came out of the suit. He arranged the tree branches in a way and attempted to light them on fire using the lighter that he had. He tried and tried again, but the logs didn't catch fire. Vivek looked on, shaking.

"Damn it!! Burn you stupid log!"

"That's not how you do it." Vivek remarked, getting up and putting whatever little strength he had into the effort. "You need tinder first, you can't just expect to light a whole log on fire using that small lighter." Vivek bent off and broke the small twigs of the logs and tore part of his under shirt while placing it in the middle, he lit small piece of cloth and upon it placed the small twigs. They slowly caught fire and without letting the fire die away. Blowing air into fire at times, he kept adding the twigs, gradually increasing the size of the pieces of wood. In about 20 minutes, the fire started going steady and Vivek backed off with Arjun looked visibly helpless but impressed. Vivek lay back down close to the fire and closed his eyes.

"That was impressive" Arjun said while coming closer to the fire himself.

"What can I say? I was a boy scout. They trained us for situations like these."

"No but still, I wouldn't have known how to start it."

"That's fine." Vivek mumbled, his body slowly started warming up and he was feeling better every second.

"What do we do tomorrow?"

"I was thinking about the same thing." Vivek replied with his eyes closed

"This sucks so bad." Arjun said as he carefully added another pie ce of wood to the fire.

"This cave, who would have guessed that we would be here. Maybe this cave hasn't been used for years, maybe generations. I have read about the old Silk Road that passed through here, travellers took refuge in caves, brought their own tents. This is what it must have felt like."

Arjun looked over at Vivek a little confused.

"Those people, I didn't give it another thought till now, the silk, the dyes, the medicine. Do you know gunpowder was also brought the same way?"

"No, I didn't know that, why is that important though?"

"Gunpowder changed the world. Fights went from swords and lances, to Cannon's and Muskets. Eventually to small firearms that one could carry around in a pocket and now you. Somehow seems ironic that one of the world's most advanced pieces of weaponry in the world finds its way back on the same road that gunpowder started its journey so many centuries ago."

Arjun chuckled.

"You have a very interesting view about things"

"So I have been told, not always in the good way.

They both had a moment of silence.

"I can't get Arun out of my head." Vivek spoke finally.

"Your..umm Blind friend?"

"The way those bastards picked him up and made him move. My blood was boiling; I should have at least said something, done something. All he heard was my silence. Its eating me up inside"

"It's not your fault"

"It is, He is helpless right now. At their mercy and I am the one responsible for it. It's my fault he is here in the first place. I deeply regret bringing him out here."

"That girl? Rohan kept screaming at you about. What's your story there?"

"My story?"

"Yes, your story? Obviously she means a lot to you doesn't she?"

"Means a lot me? I don't know. Who knows really? All I know is I am drawn to her."

"That's a strong word"

"Don't you have a girl?"

Arjun looked into the fire and simply smiled.

"So there is one?" Vivek lifting his body up from the ground using elbows.

"It doesn't matter. Its ancient history" Vivek remembered his definition of ancient history and smiled inside.

"How did you two meet?"

"I met her almost a year ago. I was trekking up a fort called Harishchandragad, it was tough climb and after that, we camped in the night at the top of the fort. There was another group who had come in the night. It was morning when I got up and noticed the other tents. Now there is a feature that is called Kokankada, the clouds gather up there and it's a beautiful display of the mountain interacting with the clouds. It forms a sight that most never experience. She was talking photos of a group when she saw me. I looked at her and was instantly mystified. Something in her eyes drew me towards her. One of the people there asked me to click a photograph of the entire group, so she could also join them. I walked over and took the camera from her. She seemed so beautiful; I almost forgot to take the picture. I had to be reminded by the group." Vivek let out a muted laugh and so did Arjun. "She seemed a little uncomfortable about me, I have this small problem in regards to starting at people."

"Yeah, you do." Arjun seconded

"In any case, both groups descended together and both groups started having small talk. I tried talking to her, but suddenly she seemed in a rush to get down. I admit, I must have come across as creepy but the way she bolted! Man that really broke my heart. She insisted after going down that their group get a separate bus and that was almost the last I saw of her"

"Then?"

"Well, then almost 6 months passed and I berated myself for being so creepy and bashed myself up about it, I vowed that if I ever saw her again, I would apologize. As luck would have it, I was forced by a friend from college to shoot his wedding more because he was a miser and less because I am a friend and guess who is his wife's best friend is?"

"Wow, no way!"

"Small world I suppose. I almost choked on my water when I saw her getting down along with the bride. She recognised me instantly and the feeling of disgust returned to her face. I now saw myself sticking out like a sore thumb, she immediately whispered something into my friend's wife's ear and I saw her face going bad too. I almost thought of getting away, before I was snatched by my friend and asked to take a photo of all of them together. I let out an uneasy smile after looking at all of them through the camera and asking them to smile."

"That must have been something" Arjun said laughing.

"Oh, you have no idea of the torture I faced."

"What then?"

"I went around, trying to avoid her and clicking shots of everybody but not in her direction. She suddenly appeared out of nowhere and started her interrogation.

"Aren't you the same guy on Harishchandragad?"

"No, Harishchandragad? What's that?" I said

"No, it is you. You are the creepy man"

"No, I am not creepy. It's just that you caught my eye and I couldn't keep my attention off you."

"Ewww. That's even creepier"

"Oh, I am sorry; I didn't mean it or anything."

"I thought so, I told my friend that you looked like a familiar pervert, wait till uncle and my dad hear about this."

"Oh shit, no, no, no. Wait I sorry, it's just this stupid thing I do" I tried my best to calm her down.

"What happened next?" Arjun asked intently listening

"Well, she played a prank on me. The thing is she had already asked my friends wife about me. They told her that I was basically a nice guy with some eccentric habits, so she decided to pull a fast one on me."

"Damn!"

"Damn! Is right, I almost had a heart attack. We kept meeting each other casually with my friend and wife when we went out for dinners and stuff, till I finally had the courage to ask her out on a date a few weeks ago. That's when she said yes, and then invited me on a plan to come to Ladakh and I asked her if I could take Arun along as well."

"Awesome story"

"What about you?"

"Nothing worth mentioning, there were girls in college, office romances, all of those. No one really clicked and I guess it didn't matter that much. It was always career first for me."

"I suppose that's OK too."

"Look I don't want to disappoint you or something but your friend Arun. I am not sure he can make this distance. It's too much for a guy like him"

"No, he is going to make it. I have to believe that. I owe him that much. It can't let end like this. I can't let it."

"I wonder what they would be doing right now"

A few kilometres away, the masked men kept furious pace, and forced their captives to do the same. Arun was ready to give out and Riya had never walked so hard in her life, coupled with the high altitude.

"What a couple of weaklings, 50 kilometres a day is hardly something that should affect you" Number 2 said with disdain.

"They don't do it everyday Number 2."

"You are getting suspiciously soft Number 1"

"No, you are being irrational lately."

Arun fell down with a thud, he took in heavy breaths and laid on the ground. Riya immediately crouched down to help him, she was holding his shirt and tried to ask him several times if he was ok. Number 2 came in close and asked her to move aside. He prodded him with his boot and asked him to get up. Riya and Number 1 watched with a little anger to the treatment of Arun.

"Get up you useless piece of meat."

"No, no more! Shoot me. Shoot me now" Arun said "Shoot me but I am not talking another step."

"Why do these people always need motivation?" Number 2 said with a sigh.

He walked up towards Riya and slapped her hard. He pulled her hair and punched her in the stomach till she screamed and fell to the ground holding her stomach and crying. Arun immediately reached out for her but number 2 slapped his hand. This continued for a minute where Number 2 repeatedly took to beating Riya and continuing to push Arun around.

"OK, OK I'll walk" Arun screamed as tears started flowing down his cheeks.

"Now that wasn't too difficult was it? Why did you make me do that if you were always going to agree in the end?

"Fuck you! Fuck you!"

"Watch your language there, you know this boot can be even more effective when I want it to."

Riya lay in the ground as Arun, trying to feel the ground made his way towards her. He felt responsible for what had happened. He cradled her head into his lap and asked her if she was ok. Riya was still crying from the experience and there number 2 stood not a few steps away laughing at this scene.

"Come on! We don't have all night"

"Give us a few minutes, we promise we shall move again" Arun said, his voice almost choked

"Fine, Number 1 get that heat pack out"

They all sat down with number 1 removing a small pack from his bag, he cracked the small glass separator plate in the middle of the pack which allowed the contents of the 2 halves to mix, the chemical inside glowed brightly and heat radiated from it. They rounded a few rocks up and made everyone sit in a circle. Number 2 still looked at Riya and smiled ever so often. Riya by now had not recovered from the encounter a few minutes ago. Number 1 was growing increasingly concerned about the mental stability of the man; in his mind he had made a decision, as soon as this was over. There would be one more mysterious death.

35

"Do you think I am a fool?"

"I am telling you that a giant metal man fell on the top of my car!"

"What about these bullet holes?"

"This man is either crazy or not telling the truth." the Jawan mentioned to his comrade standing next to him

"What's that over there?" asked a man dressed shabbily. The small white hair in this full head of hair, betrayed his age and the constant smoking made his fingers discoloured. He stood there, evenly fitting in with the surroundings; no one gave him another glance.

"Some nut trying to cook up a story" said the man standing next to him

"What the hell happened here?" he exclaimed as he moved in slowly around the vehicle.

"He must have been smuggling something and the vehicle got attacked by either the BSF of the Army"

"No kidding, the army doesn't play around!"

He saw a girl also standing with the man, she stood timid and on edge, there wasn't a lot of talking she was doing. She tried speaking every now and then but was turned down every time by the burly man in the uniform trying to talk to what appeared to be her driver. She was pushing her phone towards the man, again and again. Finally after their conversation was over, the man left them alone, probably to make some calls and get some orders about how to proceed. He then proceeded cautiously and trying to avoid eye contact with anyone present.

"Hi! What happened to you guys, are you OK"

"These people won't believe us! I am telling the truth"

"Which is?"

"We were attacked! First by a Giant metal man and then by 2 other men who wore masks"

"Really?"

"Yes! Why would I lie! Look at my car! It's destroyed."

"Madam, what really happened?"

"Watch for yourself as she handed him her phone."

"Oh!" said the man as he saw the phone and the video. His eyes gleamed, his heart jumped for joy and he couldn't help but smile at the sight of the phone.

"It's all in there, we are trying to get these people to understand and start helping our friends who are stuck there"

"Do you mind sharing your story? Maybe we can help."

"As in?"

"Hi, I should have introduced myself first, my name is Zakir Abbas. I am a journalist with Channel 5 News"

Tashi and Shilpa looked at each other, stunned. And while Tashi took a step back, Shilpa immediately agreed to go on the record.

"Great! Give me 2 minutes, also could you send me this video with your blue tooth?"

"Ok"

The man almost broke into a run as he navigated the camp to look for his camera man and haul him out! He woke up his cameraman who seemed to be resting to acclimatise

"Get up! Get up! We have a scoop! Big one!"

"What kind?" his camera man said rubbing his eyes as Zakir handed him his jacket and subsequently the camera.

"Big one! There is a giant metal man"

"Like Ironman?"

"Yeah, only bigger! Now guess what! We have proof of it; some tourist caught it on video!"

The cameraman leapt to his feet as he heard that piece of information.

"Where are they?"

"Outside, unsupervised and willing to talk!"

"Let's go! Let's go now!"

Colonel Brar's Quarters

12:50 AM

The phones went off all at once, the main phone was buzzing for a long time till Brar finally looked it up. I had a single message.

"Turn on Channel 5 now!"

Brar sleepily walked over the living room and turned on the TV

"To all of you who have just joined us, we have some breaking news that has just come in. This is a Channel 5 exclusive and from our reporter Zakir Abbas who has personally investigated this story and bringing it to you live from Ladakh.

"Go ahead Zakir, you are on the air."

"Hi Rajesh, we have uncovered a shocking story here in the mountains and the high passes of the Ladakh region, its only recently that we discovered that an apparently a giant metal man is on the loose in these areas and is terrorising tourists and it seems that the army is also unaware of this fact."

"Do we have any details on this man Zakir?"

"We do, Rajesh as the viewer can see on the screen, the survivor of a recent attack filmed this in secret from her place inside a car. The Metal man had initially tried to attack her and her group of friends by jumping an enormous distance and landing on their car. "

"Some of the footage may be shocking for some of our viewers."

Brar looked wide eyed as the mobile phone footage of Arjun Joshi in the Ace played on TV and the voice of the reporter described the suit. Brar instantly reached for his phone and got in touch with some people, shouting orders to take it down and find the base where Shilpa was currently at and shut down the news piece.

"We now take you live to our correspondent Zakir Abbas who is currently on the ground with the survivors of the attack. Over to you Zakir."

"Thank you Rajesh, I am standing here with one of the survivors of the attack and the person who shot the video, Shilpa. Shilpa how are you feeling right now?"

"I am fine, I am fine right now"

"How did you survive this ordeal?"

"I hid in the car and while this man waited outside"

"So he purposefully disabled your car"

"No, he said he was escaping from something else"

"Which could be a lie, you aren't sure of that"

"No, I am not"

"Also, did he try to kill someone?"

"No, he didn't"

"But you can't know that for sure"

"No, I can't"

"Let's talk about the other people who shot at you, they wanted to kill you for sure"

"Yes."

"How do you know?"

"They shot at .us with rifles"

"Was the Metal man helping them?"

"No."

"But you can't be sure"

"Hey, how many times are you going to ask that question? I told you already that the metal man said it was an accident and he wasn't helping the other people who shot at us. He helped us start our car as well."

"No I am just trying to ascertain if he is dangerous and up till now, we don't know for sure do we?"

"No, I guess not."

While they spoke, the camera man shot the vehicle at various angles often focusing on the bullet holes and the ripped open hood of the car. Brar looked helplessly as the images played on TV again and again in a loop till finally the connection was abruptly lost.

"We seem to be experiencing some technical difficulties. Please stay tuned to receive fresh updates as the story develops. However at this point it does seem that a dangerous situation is unfolding in the remote mountains to the north. We advise the people there to take precautions and move only if necessary."

Brar heaved a sigh of relief as the connection was lost; someone had finally intervened in at the base and put an end to the transmission. He knew this was bad news, someone must have stored the information somewhere, now it was a matter of strong arming the news agencies to stop the story and label it as false and accusing the channel to use sensationalism to boost its ratings. He decided that spending another moment in Delhi was useless and made arrangements for a flight to instantly take him back to the base of operations. He wanted to control this disaster before it went any more out of hand. Within half an hour, the car was ready to take him back to the airport where a small plane waited to bring him back to Leh.

Back at the base, soldiers had quickly taken all parties into custody and Shilpa and Tashi were now under constant observation, lest they do anything that would jeopardise the situation further. Shilpa and Tashi hopelessly looked at each other and Zakir was still ever observant about the activities of the Soldiers. They all were now trapped at the base.

36

The morning sun brought with it a sense of urgency for Arjun. He had blamed himself for the whole situation. He looked at Vivek and thought of what he had gone through the last day. He knew that Vivek was smart and committed to his friends, he knew he was trying to figure out the best way to escape this mess. He looked out of the cave not knowing the outcome of the day. Not knowing if he would live or die. He began having second thoughts about going to the rendezvous point. He knew that the whole plan revolved around him, if he didn't surrender the suit, the two hostages would be killed. He also was confident that if he came out of the suit and handed it over to them, they would simply kill everyone and leave. Why leave witnesses? They didn't have any leverage to counter them with, the only leverage that they had was the suit. Giving it up meant that they would lose their bargaining power. His train of thought was interrupted by Vivek who had gotten up and now moving towards him.

"Shall we leave? We still have some distance to cover before we get to the exchange point."

"I was thinking about it, should we really go?"

"What?" Vivek's expression changed

"Think about it. The only thing that is keeping them from killing your friends is the suit. I have it. Once I don't, what's stopping them from killing everybody and making off with the suit?"

"Hey, it's the only chance I have to save my friends; we are in this mess because of you. You have to help us."

"Do you really for a minute expect them to keep their word?"

"No."

"Then why do it. We can go back to the Army who must be tailing us by now"

"They may still fire"

"That's right, they MAY, they may not. Our best chance still lies in the army. They know what to do in situations like these. They have been trained for it."

"The army may be way behind us, even if they reach us, they may think that the lives of two people doesn't justify giving up the suit. From the way you described the whole thing. It looks like a secret project that the military has. They aren't going to risk it getting out in the open."

"Imagine the possibility that they are right. What will happen if we do let them get away with the suit? Wouldn't that be a failure? That would mean that we let the enemy get away with something that could change the course of the war for them"

"We aren't at war with anybody"

"No, not now, but what about 5 years from now? Do you want to compromise the security of the nation because of two people?"

"All this is really sounding an awful lot like a coward trying to run away"

"I am no Coward!"

"Yeah? Well you are coming across as one. You were on board with the whole idea; you were ok with binding Rohan till it meant that your safety could be arranged, now when it comes to my friends, you cite the national security of the country to me? And if you were that scared, why did you come this far?"

"I am rational man and I think that the security of a billion people is more important than 2 inconsequential tourists"

"Inconsequential? Did you just call the lives of 2 people Inconsequential?"

"I am telling you the facts. Don't give me that look of disgust. You know its better this way."

"Fine. Let's do it your way. Why don't you scoot back to the Army and let me wear the suit and go."

"That can't happen"

"No, then I'll simply take it"

Vivek started walking towards the suit which now lay powered down, Arjun heaved forward and stood between him and the suit. The two locked eyes and Vivek tried pushing Arjun aside. A scuffle broke out between them. Both punched and kicked as hard as they could, they weren't fighters, both inexperienced in fighting, except for Arjun, he had been in one not too long ago. The two men brawled like wrestlers, trying to counter each other's blows and trying to restrain the movements of each other. Vivek landed a few hard elbows on Arjun causing him to momentarily break away. Vivek rushed again to the suit only to have his leg pulled and causing him to drop to the ground. It was Arjun's turn to try and get up, Vivek too was quick, moving swiftly and locking his head with his elbow. Both men got up and Arjun rushed backwards causing Vivek to impact his head against the cave wall. Both men fell to the ground with Vivek nursing his head. The scuffle ended almost just as quickly as it began. Both men looked at each other with anger and contempt.

"I am not letting you take it"

"You want more? I can still go toe to toe with you." Vivek spoke his voice filled with rage.

"Do what you want. I am not letting you hand over the suit to them."

"You coward! Why did you even come?"

Both went silent as none had the advantage over the other. They looked at each other till finally Vivek spoke.

"I have a plan." Arjun looked at him as he stood up and continued

"You don't want to go and place your life in danger. Fine! Don't do that and maybe you are right. The Suit is what's keeping them from killing Arun and Riya. What if we could ensure that they both lived and the suit still go in their hands?"

"How are you going to pull that off?"

"A bait, we bait them with the suit, we keep the suit out of their reach but only barely but as soon as they have it, they won't be able to move it"

"Go on."

"We go to the exchange point but I go alone. You would hang back wearing the suit. I would tell them that until they release the Arun and Riya, they won't be getting the suit."

"Why would they listen to you?"

"We were assuming until now that they have nothing to lose, maybe they don't but this obsession behind this suit means it's important to them and that gives us the leverage. Didn't you mention that the suit is now low on power?"

"Yes, it's almost down to single digits."

"We get you to expend the suits energy and make you stand a little farther behind. Once Riya and Arun are brought back to we will tell them that they can go get the suit, as soon as you see us, you come out of the suit and simply walk away, by the time they approach the suit. The battery would be so low, that it wouldn't start or even if it did, it would take them time to figure out the controls of the machine. If they start it and try taking it out, the low power of the suit would mean that it would simply stop midway. Also the size and weight of the damn thing would ensure that they wouldn't be able to haul it on their backs."

"That could work. After all they don't know that the suit is running low on power"

"The army may be on its way but frankly we need to set up a play here before anyone else can, once they are stuck with the suit, then the army can take care of the rest, agreed?"

"Ok but the first sign of funny business and I am out of there"

"Fine, let move out now."

The duo set off into the wilderness again. The Snow began to fall again, ever so evenly. Vivek climbed on back of the suit again and prepared himself for the exchange. All the pieces were in motion, it was now or never.

37

Arun and Riya walked wearily and with every foot forward, it seemed like they would crash down. The masked men kept prodding them. Number 1 was noticeably behaving a little strange and distant. Number 2 hadn't changed his attitude. They kept pushing their hostages through the landscape. They had a massive head start on the people who were coming right now. Arun was the one who was most physically spent. His feet had developed boils and the dehydration was making his muscles cramp, he made an attempt to sit every now and then but was met only with the boot of Number 2. He would have given up long ago, if not for Riya and the threat to her life. The 4 of them reached the pre decided spot much in advance and decided it was better for them to stay hidden and wait for the others to arrive. Their training did not let them relent for one bit. They grouped Riya and Arun together and made them sit in a corner. They were confident, they didn't even bind them. Riya felt the ruthlessness of them a few hours ago and making a run for it was hardly on her mind and as for Arun, how and where would he run? The men took up positions behind boulders and waited patiently for the others to arrive.

Riya looked at Arun. All weary and broken down, she knew that it was much more than what his body could take. Riya hadn't even spoken to him for the longest time. She just accepted him as Vivek's friend. Arun finally broke the silence.

"I tried to be a rat, you know that?"

"What do you mean?"

"Since we are about to die anyway, I wanted to apologise to you"

"What for, there is nothing to apologise for, it's just fate" Riya said dejected

"No, I tried to sell you out, I became desperate."

"How did you do that?"

"I was scared and frustrated, I tried telling them to set me free and keep you instead. Knowing that Vivek would come for you. I tried; to save my own life putting you in harm's way."

Riya would have been angry and filled with rage, at this betrayal but instead she thought of the time that she tried to escape without giving him a second thought. She thought to herself how people really become desperate and selfish in their times of need and despair, no one gives a second thought to someone else. It was all so disappointing. Human nature is perhaps only about survival. The survival of the self, to save anyone else, it must first be convenient. She thought of the incident where she was stopped by the terrain and couldn't go any further. She thought back to that moment. If it was possible, would she really have escaped?

"It's fine Arun" she said.

"No it isn't, I thought only for myself. I didn't even spare a thought for your life. Is my life really more valuable than yours? I was being selfish and completely disregarded your life. I didn't care if you lived or died, as long as my skin was safe. It's eating me up inside your life, your being. You are someone's child, someone's sister, someone's beloved, someone's friend. I am disgusted with myself for doing that. Please, please forgive me."

Arun's words were eating up the both of them inside. They were like poison arrows as Riya realised that everything that Arun was saying was doubly true for her. Here was this unfortunate man who had been kicked around by life and still he felt genuinely sorry. She hadn't been feeling sorry for him but now, she started feeling sorry for herself. It was even more infuriating for her because she didn't have the strength to admit to Arun, what he was admitting to her. She didn't have the strength to tell him that she was about to leave him for dead if she was not stopped by the mountains. In those few moments, she felt the smallest she had ever felt in her life. There wasn't a word she could say, so she collected her thoughts and continued to sit calmly

"You think Vivek is coming?" she finally asked

"No doubt, he is on his way"

"What about the other guy? Do you think Vivek could have convinced him to come along?"

"Even if that guy isn't here. Vivek will be here."

"Without the other guy, only him showing up would be useless wouldn't it, he might as well not come and save himself"

"He doesn't think like that. He will show. For sure and mark my words, he will have some plan"

"Some plan?"

"The problem with other people is that they don't understand what Vivek is capable of. His mind is a sharp; you never exactly know what's going on in there. You have met him, you must have some hint."

"He is smart, that much I know for sure."

"Just you wait; he will have something up his sleeve."

They waited like that for a few hours, till finally number 2 was alerted by a silhouette, it was a single man. He took out his monocular and saw Vivek slowly walking towards them. The Suit was nowhere to be seen. He called for number 1 and asked him to scout the area, he took his own monocular and in the distance, on a rock face the ACE came into view. He wasn't moving. This vexed the two masked men.

"Is he trying to pull something off here?" Number 2 asked.

"I don't know"

"Tell him to stop."

"Right there is fine!" shouted Number 1. Vivek froze. He didn't see them, they were talking from cover."

"Move slowly and come in this direction." Vivek obeyed.

"No! Don't let him come here! Ask him why the other guy isn't with him" whispered number 2

"Stop! Why isn't the other man with you? No suit, no deal"

"You will get your suit." Vivek shouted

"No games, we will kill everyone right now!"

"You will get your suit when you have set these people free. Once we are satisfied that no harm will come to us, you can take the damned thing and do what you want with it."

"You don't make the rules, we do! And we say the suit comes here right now."

"If you want it, then let them go, he will abandon the suit there and you can go get it."

"Are you still thinking this is a discussion?" Number 2 spoke as he went in the back, caught Riya by the back of her neck and brought her forward. Riya squirmed and struggled as she stood before Vivek.

"You get him down, right now! Or we shoot this bitch!"

"Don't!" Vivek reacted instantly

"Oh yes, this one is special isn't she?" number 2 laughed as he tightened his grip around Riya's neck making her scream.

"If you harm her! You won't get it. Let her and my other friend go and you can have what you want."

"No negotiations! Bring him down here"

"I guess then it's just a matter of who wants what more. I am not moving from here till you let everyone go and the suit isn't coming down. No matter what do. You might as well kill everybody right now if you aren't going to move from your position. He sees that we are dead. He runs. Bye bye suit, you get me?"

"If you leave with the suit, what then? That man is standing so far off."

"Of course, it's our insurance"

"We are supposed to take your word for it, is it? How do we know that he won't run off?"

"We are supposed to take your word for it? How do we know you won't kill us all when you have what you need?"

Vivek was doing an awful lot of posturing for someone who was scared as baby kitten on the inside. Arun listened to the voice of the two men going back and forth. He too was filled with fear and the consequences of this very confrontation but he was thankful that Vivek thought of something before he came here, that was like the man he knew. The masked men had lost their advantage, they had assumed that this would be a simple thing to do. Once they had the suit, they would have killed everyone and made off with it. Now however there was a unique problem. One they hadn't counted on. They couldn't have the suit till everyone was free and that went against everything that they stood for. Avoid detection at all costs, even if it means giving up on something they want. That was their motto. The two men exchanged as they faced with a problem they weren't expecting. They had relied on the fear of these men and now that backfired. Number 1 looked again at Vivek who was standing a few feet away while he made his decision. In his mind, it was clear.

"Shoot them." he said plainly and calmly without raising or changing the tone of his voice, he always had.

"What? Shoot them? Then we can't get the suit"

"Doesn't matter. Whether or not we get the suit is immaterial"

"We went through a lot of trouble for this Number 1; do you expect that we would simply abandon it now that it is within reach?"

"Avoid detection, at all costs, even if we have to give up everything, even our lives. Those are the words we live by, or have you forgotten?"

"Again going Idealistic, stop making excuses, we simply walk to that place"

"Shoot them or I will" came the quick reply, Number 1 wasn't interested in debates or conversations.

"No, I am not going to shoot them and you better start learning to stay in your limits."

Number 1 went for his guns calmly, as soon as his partner saw that, he let Riya go, kicked her to the side and trained his rifle on him. Number 1 was now shocked beyond belief. A team member had pulled a weapon on him. The expressions on his face changed, the usually calm and collected man had rage burning through his eyes, his teeth slowly showed themselves. If there wasn't a gun trained at him. He would have killed Number 2 right then and there.

"Put that down! How dare you!"

"Shut up! I have had enough of your self-righteous bullshit. I am taking over command now. You will follow my orders from now on!"

"You will pay for this!"

"Didn't I tell you? I am the hand of God here. Nothing of his will is done, except through me"

Both Riya and Arun were baffled by the turn of events. Vivek stood dumbfounded, not knowing what to speak. In the distance Arjun looked at everything and assumed that something had gone very, very wrong. Unknown to all of them, Apollo and his team were watching the scene with great interest. No one knew that they were there. They were stealthily getting closer and closer not giving themselves away, they came by from their right side, and the commotion was just the diversion they needed to catch them off guard. Vivek's plan was somewhat coming together, some variables had changed but he was still confident of the outcome. He had just managed to get all the pieces in the right places. He looked on at Number 1 as he was being moved away from the hostages.

"So, let's talk about what is going to happen next" number 2 said letting out a smile.

38

Life in the army is boring if you lack discipline and you tend to be a day dreamer. Patrolling the high passes and the vast plains in the awful temperature is one of those things you certainly don't like, if you don't have the stomach for adventure. The young man broke away from his patrolling unit as he went to relive himself. He still wasn't used to the high altitude of this place, he was part of a new batch of recruits that was sent to the mountains and his unit was sent out with the veterans on an acclimatisation run. The veterans made fun of his lanky build and even managed to get his purse which had a picture of his sweetheart. He remembered his village on the banks of the Yellow river as he sat down, the village had a bad fishing season the pollution from the factories up river was killing the fish. Bad luck meant that what he would have to go serve in the Army to ensure that they still had enough to eat. Without a good education, the army was the only way out.

While his thoughts took him back home on the banks of the great river. His eyes caught a sight that he wasn't expecting to see. He buttoned up his pants and rushed furiously to his unit which was a few meters away.

"Sir! Sir! There is movement on the other side!"

"Calm down, The Indians have their patrols the same as us"

"It's not a patrol!"

"They are pointing their weapons! There is also something shiny that

I can't make out"

"You are positive?"

"Come see for yourself Sir."

The unit commanders face was now covered in concern. They weren't supposed to be here at this time, this was a surprise run and Intelligence had not alerted them of any activity. He looked from across the border with his binoculars. The soldier was right. He could see army personnel in getting ready to attack and on the other side, it looked strange. He wasn't sure of what to make of it.

"Get me base! Right now! I want some orders!"

The soldier returned with the communications trained soldier of the group. His eyes were peeled on the movement of the soldiers while he waited for his unit commander to respond.

"Go ahead"

"Sir, we are seeing a build-up of soldiers in area 43. The soldiers seem ready to move but haven't noticed our patrol yet. Advice further action"

"How many are there?"

"Not many, it seems like a specialized unit. From their stance, it does seem that they are waiting to move on something."

"If they cross or even attempt to cross, shoot them! This must be an attempt to infiltrate our territory"

"Sir, we have mostly new recruits in this team. I would like to request backup as soon as possible"

"You will have it."

"Thank you sir, over and out."

The small unit made up of mostly boys took their positions and had the Indians in sights, they had an advantage, the Indians didn't know of their presence. The officer slowly arranged the men into positions to get the enemy into over lapping lines of fire. The boys tried hard to remember their training and while they tried to hold still, some of their rifles shook as much as they did. The officer tried hard to motivate them to stay calm. The entire line stood ready and focused.

"Fire on my order" the officer said.

On the other side, Apollo realised this was the time to strike, he signalled his team to slowly move forward , while the two men were fighting amongst themselves, they had gained a lot of ground taking advantage of the ruckus. He raised his hand and put up 3 fingers, and made a circular motion, meaning he wanted three soldiers to move into another position, covering the target from behind. As three soldiers instantly got up and made their way to their left, one of them fell to the ground with a bullet in his arm, moments later the sound of a gunshot echoed all around them.

The boy had let out a shot; the boy from the banks of the Yellow river had fired his first shot towards the enemy. He shook with fear and gave a blank expression when his officer looked at him. Vivek, the masked men, Arjun, Apollo, Riya and Arun heard the echo of the gunshot, all of them dumbfounded by the implications. The Jawan right next to the one, who was shot, lost his composure and started firing bursts into the direction of the gunshot!

"Fire" was the order from the Chinese officer.

Confusion ruled as both the Indian and the Chinese side opened fire on each other completely ignoring the situation going on below and the mountains echoed with the sounds of machine gun fire and mayhem ensued. Instantly Arjun moved from his position, the ACE reading enhanced neural information accelerated him to where the action was on. Number 1 looked to take advantage of the situation and reached for his gun. Number 2 saw the moment and rapidly fired at Number 1. He dodged the fire and moved quickly to the side. Letting out a few rounds in the process. Number 2 quickly followed up with his own barrage of fire. Number 2 tried to run along quickly in the direction of where Number 1 was going as Riya quickly moved in and caught him by his legs causing him to fall to the ground and landing on his rifle. He tried kicking her aside and finally with the full force of his legs and was finally successful. He noticed the rifle, it was bent. He threw it away as he removed his handgun and looked for Number 1. Number 1 caught up with Arun and was using him as a shield.

"Remember, if he dies, you don't get what you want"

"That is if he dies." with that, Number 2 shot Arun in the leg causing him to scream loudly in pain. Number 1 quickly pushed Arun towards number 1 and managed to knock his handgun out. The two wrestled in the on ground with and both separated from each other. They drew out their knives as they circled each other like animals and went at it again. Both fought with ferocity, until in a decisive move, Number 2 faked going left, moved to his right and plunged the knife deep into his opponents thigh. Number 1 tried to counter with his blade but missed his target. He stood back limping and holding his wound. He came back around and now with the advantage completely his, he grabbed number 1 arm that held the knife and repeatedly stabbed him in the stomach with great speed. The ferocity and the strength at which he moved send shivers down the spine of Riya and Vivek. The blood stained white clothes looked very different from before. Number 2 let the body go as it fell to the ground and blood pooled around his corpse. Number 2 spat on the lifeless body and kicked it a few times but as he turned, he saw the giant ACE almost upon him, closing the distance with a great speed. He rushed for his handgun which was lay just a few steps away, he reached it in time, cocked it and fired consecutive shots at point blank range at the charging behemoth. It was no use, the armour was too thick. Arjun slammed the ACE into his body and he was flung away. He made quick work of his handgun and proceeded to hit him with his giant metal arms as he was still on the ground. Number 2 had his hands full. His face now had now opened up and blood flowed out from under the mark turning the mask red. With a final strike, Number 2 lay motionless on the ground.

Vivek hurried to Riya as she was lying on the ground, she raised her hands and placed them around him as she cried her heart out. Vivek kissed her forehead and reassured her that he was right there and he was going to check on Arun. He found him writing in pain and made himself known before he walked to him.

"Arun! It's me Vivek!"

"About fucking time you showed up" he let out successive cries of pain as he held his palms over his wound"

"Are you going to be ok?"

"What does it look like?"

"I don't know. Just keep pressure on it. It will stop the bleeding"

"Could you not repeat the same dialogue about a gunshot wound that's in every damn movie?"

"Glad to see you again Arun!" Vivek chuckled as he realised the ordeal was over and sat down right next to Arun. Riya walked up to him and sat down in front of him.

"Is it over?"

"Yes. It's over."

The firing too had stopped. Apollo made his way swiftly to the location of the others and saw them sitting on the ground and the ACE standing next to a motionless body. The soldiers trained their guns on the ACE.

"Oh no! Not this again!" Arjun said remembering what had happened the last time.

"Lower your weapons" Apollo ordered

"It's fine, come out."

Arjun started the exit protocol and came out of the ACE. The soldiers surrounded him. Vivek came out seeking medical assistance for Arun. Two jawans rushed in to help Arun.

"So you must be Vivek."

"Yes Sir."

"Good idea to leave your friend like that. We could have shot him"

"It's nice of you to not shoot him Sir." Vivek chuckled as he remembered the protests and the foul words Rohan screamed at them as Arjun and Vivek bound him and covered him in Rocks.

"Who are they and why did we get fire from across the border?"

"I don't know sir. They asked us to meet them here in order to do the exchange; we simply assumed they needed to get out of India."

"This other guy isn't dead, I simply knocked him out. He can tell you things as long as you can make him talk" Arjun added.

"Oh we will make him talk; we will make him into a storyteller"

"I hope no one was grievously injured in the fight."

"Well, we have a soldier with a gunshot wound to his arm, that's about it. I don't know about the other side. They must have had some losses as they stopped firing."

"I wonder what exactly happened here." Vivek said as he looked to the other side.

His attention was slowly caught by a faint buzzing which grew louder every second. He looked to his back and saw three dots slowly growing larger. Within a few seconds, the roar of helicopters was heard. The Helicopters landed at a little distance away from them and out poured troops with their faces covered. They quickly took up positions around the site and as soon as the last one took his spot. Hades himself stepped out of the helicopter. The Soldiers including Apollo stood fast and presented smart salutes. The Colonel looked glaringly at Arjun who looked down to the ground as he couldn't meet his gaze. He looked at Apollo and remarked.

"Good Job, Son"

On the other side. The firing was almost stopping; the Chinese side had stopped firing and were now in full retreat. The Chinese officer looked at the face of the young soldier now being carried on a stretcher; a bullet had hit his lower chest. His lungs were filling up with blood. The officer reassured him with encouraging words as he kept repeating the name of his beloved in the delirium. The Officer called on for his communications man.

"Sir, we encountered a very heavily armed enemy force, they were armed to the teeth with weapons that we haven't faced before. This is bad."

"Did you stop their advance?"

"At great cost sir, we did. The enemy isn't advancing and we seemed to have checked their movement. We have a lot of injured, some which might not make it Sir. "

"They will pay Captain. They will pay"

39

The Prime Minister's office

12:40 PM, New Delhi

The phone rings several times as the Prime minister isn't interested in picking up a call and interrupting his meeting with the Turkish minster of Commerce. He signals his PA to the telephone. The PA quickly answers the phone, tells plainly that the Prime minster is busy and slams the phone right back again without listening to a word. The phone rings again and the PA answers the phone again, this time trying to tell the staff in a more stern manner that no calls are important as of right now. Before he can continue his rant, the answer from the other side immediately makes him stop and pay attention, after a few seconds. He meekly moves towards the Prime Minister with the receiver in hand and stands right behind him.

"Sir," he speaks almost in a whisper.

"Sir." he speaks again, louder after clearing his throat.

"What?" the Prime Minister turns,

"Sir you need to take this call, it's quite urgent."

"Mr Prime Minster, We have been talking for quite some time, let's stop for now and resume after lunch?"

"Sure, Minister. Please, I will join you momentarily."

The minster walked out of the room as the prime minster glared at his PA.

"I told you no disturbances during the meeting; Iw was just about to crack the biggest deal there!"

"Sir, just please listen." The PA pleaded as he moved the receiver over to him

"Give me the phone."

The prime ministers face also lost colour as he heard the news. He turned to his PA and said almost in shock.

"Cancel the meeting with the Minister, Call for an immediate meeting with the Defence minister and the Chiefs of the forces. Inform the President."

The PA rushed out dialling numbers his mobile phone in frenzy. The Prime minister waited in his office and checked the news channels for any news of the current situation. The word travelled quickly around Luytens Delhi. The Armed forces buildings saw an unusual frenzy as the top brass were glued to their phones and giving orders back into them. The cars with the three Services chiefs arrived at the Prime Minister's office and the Defence minister was summoned from his meeting elsewhere. The four men made it to the armed forces WAR room where they all sat and talked amongst each other. The Prime Minister came in and everybody stood up. With a gesture of his hands, he asked everyone to sit down and took a seat himself at the middle of the table.

"Gentlemen what is going on? I do not expect to be informed of such news on the phone in this way"

"Sir, this was most unexpected." The Army chief spoke "The Chinese have opened fire on all the border positions in the Ladakh region. There isn't a single one that is not under fire. All the Checkpoints have been evacuated and regular activity that we see from them is gone."

"What does this suggest?"

"The way their aircraft are mobilizing and being send to Forward bases in the Tibet region, I'd say they are preparing for a first strike" The Air force chief added

"First strike? Over what? Relations have never been so warm. I even visited China Last month."

"Sir, there seems to be a disconnect between the leadership and the armed forces. Intelligence has been suggesting that the Chinese generals have been trying to become more autonomous in their operations. We have intercepts that show many generals expressly disobeying orders from Party leaders and going ahead with whatever they want" The defence ministers tone was worrying and the Prime minister and the other chiefs looked shocked over this revelation.

"Why weren't any of the Armed forces told?"

"There was no need to, the intelligence agencies report directly to me. Also they didn't think it was a problem at that time."

"Typical"

"Wait a minute" The Prime minster said "Are you saying, they are going to invade?"

"Yes sir, a co-ordinated attack like this points in only one direction. They got Aksai Chin in the 60's now it looks as they want all Ladakh"

"No, no, I need to speak to the Chinese premier"

"Sir, we need to mobilise troops to the region and get the Air Force ready to respond"

"You do that."

"Sir there may also be something else." The Prime ministers PA spoke. "Last night there was a strange request from the army. One of the officers requested a trace on a particular individual. The officer is part of the Black Units; we know that they are active in that area. Should we check with them?"

The Prime minister looked at the Army chief expecting an answer. He looked back at everyone and shook his head and said the Black units are black because they don't report directly to him; they are part of the Defence minsters responsibilities. The entire table now looked towards the Defence minister.

"He hasn't reported anything in months, although I shall check with him"

"Go ahead, call him here right now." The Prime Minister ordered. "As for the current mess, please go ahead and try calling the Chinese premier for me."

The PA rushed outside as the call was made for Brigadier Bakshi a.ka. Kronos. He got the call while still sitting at his desk, he knew what had happened and although Brar hadn't checked in quite some time, he knew that it was something that could have happened because the place Brar was going was very close to LAC. He readied himself as he wore his cap and adjusted his Coat. His phone buzzed.

"Mission successful

Prototype recovered,

Civilians unhurt,

Enemy combatant captured,

Reporting fire on rendezvous position from the Chinese side."

He was on top of the entire story, even if Brar didn't tell him what he wanted to hear, his eyes and ears were everywhere. You don't get to be the boss of the spooks without being a spook yourself. The Car drove quickly with an escort and arrived the meeting. He knocked the door before he came in and presented his salutes to the people in the room. He took his seat in front of all the other members in the room.

"What's happening Brigadier?" the Defence Minster spoke, "It this any of your men?"

"Sir. The other people in the room don't have the clearance to listen to what I am about to say"

"Don't worry about clearance now. Just go ahead, we have an emergency situation." The prime minster said, hoping for an explanation to the events of the day.

"With all due respect Sir, It is you who don't have the clearance for this information Sir"

The Prime Minsters mouth opened with Shock, the highest elected official in the country of over a billion people, does not have access? It hit his Ego hard and strong.

"I am sorry Sir, its protocol, also it shield you. Plausible deniability" The Defence Minster spoke

"I think we can suspend that for now, don't you think Minister?" The Prime Minister smiled deviously.

"Yes, Yes. Of course Sir. Brigadier please continue"

The brigadier took a deep breathed before continuing

"After the Kargil conflict, and losing many soldiers to the cross border fire, it was decided in late 2003 to have a program that would help enhance our soldier's effectiveness in Combat, especially in places where we had a disadvantage. The steep climbs in the Mountains of Kargil and the Cold took a lot out of our boys. The increasing threat of China's presence in the South China Sea and its ever increasing sphere of influence worried us; as well the quick response times to Pakistan's Jets on the Western front remained an issue"

"Not to interrupt you Brigadier, but just a question, what is Pakistan doing currently? Is it talking advantage of this situation?"

"No, it doesn't seem so sir. There has been sporadic firing but nothing concrete to speak of."

"Fine, continue."

"As I was saying, we needed quick, easy and fast responses to the problems and for that reason. Project Trident was born. We divided the three heads into the three Greek Gods of the Olympian Trinity, one for the Army, One for the Navy and one for the Air force. Their Heads are called Hades, Poseidon and Zeus. They are all responsible for shaping the next generation of covert and regular operatives and eventually leading the entire Army into the acceptance of their methods and technology"

The table listened with great interest as the brigadier went on.

"We contract Indian Technology companies with above average credentials to build custom technology for us under strict privacy and supervision. One of those products was the ACE or the advanced combat enhancer. It's designed as a suit to enhance the combat faculties of a soldier tenfold while enhancing his defensive capabilities tremendously. A couple of Days ago, Hades, the Army head, was contacted by a person called Arjun Joshi, who works for one of the firms that manufacture our suits. According to Hades, the man went rogue and killed two soldiers at his base and then fled the scene, in all probability to escape with the technology and give it to the Chinese or anyone who would pay good money for it. The plot thickened yesterday when it was discovered that several people of unknown origin were spotted by the units sent after Joshi in a attempt to recover the suit.

"What happened next?" The Prime minister inquired with his hands now folded and leaning back in his chair.

"It was later discovered that the people surrounding the suit as traced by the Army units were a mixture of Indian civilians, most likely tourists and 2 others of unknown origins but not civilians for sure. It seemed that the 2 people had kidnapped some of the civilians and demanded the suit in exchange for their lives. That drama ended today morning when a crack group of elite officers and Jawans were sent after the civilians, ending the crisis and putting the suit back into our hands. It remains to be seen if Joshi was guilty of anything. One of the unknown's is in custody. The Civilians also seem unhurt for the most part. Although one of the reports that came out of the area, report a cross border fire fight with Chinese. It is my opinion that there was some confusion the site, since it was extremely close to the LAC and the Chinese might have opened fire thinking that were about to pull off some stunt. "

"So this could all be a misunderstanding?" The Prime Minister asked

"Yes Sir, it's possible."

"Ok, now I definitely need to speak to the Chinese premier."

"Sir, the information I have shared is deemed above top secret and on a very strict need to know basis. May I remind you that you may not share any such details with a foreign military organisation that may jeopardise the safety of our soldiers."

"Relax Brigadier; I know how to deal with this. I am not the Prime Minister for nothing and next time you people decide to have your little secrets, make sure I am invited to the party."

"Brigadier, if I could ask you," asked the Navy chief, do you mean there are versions of the machine designed for the Navy?"

"Yes Sir, there is a version of the ACE designed for Sea warfare as well versions designed for Air Warfare"

"Well, this is amazing, I didn't know about this."

"We are proud that you don't know about this of that Sir."

"Who is Poseidon?"

"That Identity is withheld Sir."

"In any case, get your men to calm down and think rationally. Hold them back for God's sake. We don't want another war with China. Let all the investigations take their time, no Rash moves"

There was an authority in the voice of the defence minister's voice. Brigadier Bakshi got up saluted the office of the Prime minister and left.

40

"In retrospect, I wouldn't take this trip again."

"Shut up Arun."

"Look at the bright side, now you all can experience what it feels like to be blind!"

"Shut up Arun!", now there were multiple voices."

"Ok."

"He really needs to learn to be appropriate"

"Yeah, he does"

The air was thin outside, but this was different, it wasn't the mountain any more. The black bags on their head made it impossible to see, but flying is an experience that does not need to be seen to know instinctively. The sudden change in speed, take off, the change in Air pressure as the ears pop. Pretty unmistakable signs that they were flying. They had been for several hours. No one knew where they were going. They only knew about the bags on their heads as soon as that Colonel descend from that helicopter and forced them into the helicopter and then into a plane.

Vivek whispered to Arjun,

"Hey, any ideas?"

"Nope, I have no clue."

"Why do you think they are doing this?"

"Frankly, I sort of think it was because of me, or rather because you all saw me"

"So it continues."

"I am sorry."

"No, I was actually a little surprised, you told me in the morning that you wouldn't come and help us but you did. I wasn't expecting that."

"I couldn't just stand by any more and I had the power, so why not?"

"Speaking of power, how many per cent was left?"

"None the emergency power kicked in when I was standing on the rock there. If it wasn't there. Then things would have been different."

"So, I guess they finally did install that emergency power"

"Guess they did."

"Riya, are you ok?"

"No. Is there anything in the last 2 days that makes you think I would be ok?"

"Hey, I was just asking you a question"

There was only silence from her. The plane hardly yawed or banked. It was a long flight. They finally detected that the plane was losing altitude and was preparing to land. They prepared for the landing. Military flights are very different from commercial airliners. They don't feel the same way at all. As soon as the flight landed, they were escorted from a plane into a Bus and while they waited for the bus to move, there was another familiar sound that they all heard.

"Can you please tell me why this bag is over my head? Please I demand to know"

"Hi Rohan"

"Is that you Vivek?"

"Yup! Say hello to Arjun, Arun and Riya as well"

"Riya!!!! Riya!!! Where are you?"

"I am right here Rohan."

"Are you ok? Oh my god you made it."

"Yes, I am fine" Vivek rolled his eyes from inside his bag

"I have been so concerned about you. I was worried sick!"

The conversation between Rohan and Riya seemed never ending. The bus eventually started moving and in a short time they could hear the sea and the waves crashing on the rocks. They soon realised they were a long way from where they originally began. Vivek tried talking to the driver or anyone else in the bus but no one paid attention. They were just along for the ride. After around half an hour in the bus, they were hauled out and made to stand in a line, they were lead down a path, then an Elevator and finally when they reached their destination. It was underground, that they knew for sure. Their masks were finally taken off and in front of them, stood Colonel Brar.

"We have transported you this secure facility for your own protection. We are still ascertaining if this man here, Joshi is a criminal and a traitor to his country, it also goes without saying that you too are in the realm of suspicion as you have been seeing moving around with him."

"Can you get off your high horse? Who gave you the right to put such allegations?" Arjun demanded "What right do you have placing us under such conditions, how can you keep a straight face and say that we are here for our protection." he had had enough of him, enough of his high handedness.

"I say your protection, because, if I would have left you back at the base, the soldiers would have killed you for killing their comrades." the Colonel squinted his eyes at him

"Sir, we are innocent and have been trapped up in this. We have nothing to do with National Security and anything of the sort really, me and my friends here, simply wish to be released and be free of this nightmare that we have been facing. Look at her face sir. Does this look like a face of a traitor or a conspirator to you? No sir, She has been battered by the very man we helped bring down today."

"Let them go Brar, they have nothing to do with this." Arjun said as he looked away

"I make the decisions around here." he replied almost instantly

The colonel moved around till he got masked man who had arrived retrained to a bed. He pulled out his bloodied mask and inside, the face of a beat down man showed itself. The beating he got from the ACE was apparent. His eyes and cheek were swollen while blood had been gushing from the head. His face was unapologetic. He smiled at the Colonel.

"Take him to the Infirmary, make sure he watched at all times, no exceptions"

Another man in sharp navy whites came down and visited the Colonel. Arjun recognised his face from the files.

"I know him!" he whispered

"That guy?

"Yes! He was in the file. We were developing the navy version of the suit for him"

"There is a navy version of the suit too?" asked a bewildered Vivek

"As well as an Air force one"

"Well, miracles never cease"

The meeting of the two men took a strange turn as Brar returned with a grim look on his face. "Kronos is doing what he does best, he is eating his children"

"I have been ordered to let you go! Stop all activities on the borders; entrap the soldiers already fighting in their positions. It's Kargil all over again"

"Hades, Stop it, we have our orders!"

"Do you want to know, why I am what I am? It's because of men like Bakshi; it's because of weak links like him that I am supposed to lay down my soldiers!"

"I should have stopped listening to him 17 years ago. When he abandoned us and doomed us to a fate worse than death! A fate of dishonour. I live with that every day."

Brar continued for some time as he recollected the olden days. The final days of the Kargil were brutal. The fiercest conflicts of the entire war. Brar was a young captain leading his forces up a feature that was infested with enemy forces. The support was dwindling. The army couldn't keep resupplying the front line soldiers with the ammunition and the food they needed to keep going. It was at that time that a brave Navy Commando who was brought in on loan from the special forces group to teach the new soldiers some special forces moves, volunteered to support the unit but with no way to make headway into the field of battle. A helicopter pilot from the Air Force volunteered to be his shuttle. During the way, the Helicopter was shot but both men managed to escape without injury. In the coming few hours though some exceptional fighting, they pushed against overwhelming odds and managed to recapture the point back for India. It was that day that Brar received his nickname, "Hades" the God of the Underworld, his ferocity and unrelenting assaults made the enemy feel as if they were near the Gates of hell itself. The 3 men from the 3 different services fought like Gods that night, the enemy had codenamed the peak Olympus but now, they codenamed the 3 soldiers as well, the Gods of Olympus, Hades, Zeus and Poseidon.

The photograph that Bakshi had in his house was the last photo anyone took of them together Hades, Poseidon and Zeus in one frame proudly standing over the captured peak. In the coming weeks that followed, all three went from simple soldier to legends. The enemy dared not attack the same point again, fearing the wrath of the Olympian Gods. They stayed meek and defensive. But betrayal came at the hands of the very people commanding them. Bakshi had asked them to go capture another point without sufficiently guarding the one they recently captured. Their pleas fell on deaf ears and as soon as they evacuated their posts and left 4 men in charge, the enemy came back and killed everyone while recapturing the post. The post that was won with such huge odds. When there was a ceasefire, the enemy laid down hundreds of Land mines, they claimed the lives of innumerable soldiers, so many from his command that he grew weary of the command structure. He resented Bakshi for his command decisions. He was incapable of seeing the bigger picture.

"It's confirmed, the bullets that killed the Captain and other Jawan didn't come from the ACE" Poseidon said

"How did you know about the bullets?"

"Its common practice to conduct post mortems of deaths under suspicious circumstances."

"That lieutenant told you didn't he? It doesn't clear him of running; he could still be a part of it."

"Brar, that's enough, no need to take it any further. Also none of this would have happened if you hadn't forced him to get in the suit."

"How did the men know to be there? How did they know that Arjun was going to be there?"

"The initial trace by the NIA and the CBI show emails from his boss discussing Joshi's travel details, it might have been hacked by someone or instructions were then passed on those people in the masks."

"I don't believe it,"

"You don't have to, it's over. These people will be debriefed in detail and then we shall put them on the first place back home."

Brar stormed off in rage into the lower quarters. The group on top was elated, since Rohan was the first to actually arrive with them, he was the first to be let off. Arun and Riya weren't so lucky. They were grilled for hours and finally sent on their way out. It was finally the turn of Arjun and Vivek. The investigators sat in different rooms as they cross checked their answers. In the meanwhile, Colonel Brar was in his quarters when it stuck him. There was only one way he could convince them that there was a clear and present danger to the system. The only way he could do that is by showing that the system was vulnerable. The system was weak and needed improvements. He needed the help of his enemy. Something he was hoping that he could get within the rooms of the base

He got up and casually walked to the infirmary where the captured man lay. He looked at him and wondered, what if? The let the guards at the infirmary go with the pretext of interrogating him.

"What is your name?"

The man didn't respond

"You are a soldier aren't you? Not some hired gun. You still have some honour left isn't it?"

The man turned his head slightly.

"We both fight for our country, I wonder though, why didn't your country men stop shooting when they realised that you were down there? Brar paused a bit as he checked the reaction of the man.

"They didn't know you were there did they?"

The man's eyes went all around place. Making a statement.

"Yet, you still continue to stay strong? Still stay silent for that country which abandoned you?"

Brar sat in the chair next to him

"I know what it feels like, I know. I have been abandoned, they think I am crazy. So let me prove them right."

"What are you going to do?"

"Oh, so you do have a tongue. Well I am not going to ask you to do anything that you wouldn't do yourself" Brar walked towards him and placed the keys of the locks in his hand.

"There is another big suit, turn right when you come to the big door. May the best soldier win."

"Thanks"

The Colonel walked out, when he was nearing the end of the narrow lane to his quarters; he heard the screams of pain as the man now killed the two soldiers who were tasked with watching him.

"It's necessary" he said to himself as he laid down on the meagre bed and imagined what would happen in the minutes and hours to come."

41

Riya and Rohan were waiting in the upstairs common room as they flipped across the TV and stopped on the news.

"Channel 5 Correspondent Zakir Abbas is on the ground reporting from Ladakh"

"Zakir, what is going on there?"

"Rajesh, the combined firing exercise by both the governments seems to be over at this point. It was a surprise to the locals here who woke up to extremely loud gunfire and sounds of mortar explosions. It was later reported that both governments were simply finishing their own stocks of weapons which were past their expiry dates. Rajesh"

"Surely the villagers must have been scared out of their minds, Zakir"

"Some claim to know it already and have come out and commented that they knew that the government was planning an operation of the sort. We have spoken to several villagers who currently are on the border and claim that all is well between the nations. The officers have also told us that its common practice to notify other countries of exercises such as these, so they can be safe and any kind of misconception is avoided, Rajesh

"Thank you Zakir for the latest news on the ground in Ladakh."

"In other news from the region, a tourist car was fired upon a terrorist group and the driver and Passenger have survived with no injuries. The police are investigating the Issue and they hope to find leads soon.

The photo on the screen was that of Shilpa, both Riya and Rohan were left wide eyed.

"Can you believe this shit?"

"What happened?" Arun asked

"They are saying that a terrorist group fired on Shilpa and Tashi and they have miraculously escaped"

"Well stranger things can happen"

Below their feet, the alarms went off as Vivek and Arjun were still answering their prospective examiners, the lights tuned from bright white to blood red as the entire base was sent into a tizzy.

"The suit is on the loose!" Screamed a sailor as he whizzed by.

"Evacuate!" came another sound, as the sound of water started to scare everyone.

Vivek and Arjun both looked at each other and started rushing towards the main door. Which was by now crowded with Sailors and officers. Screams started coming from the back of the base and audible and Rhythmic thumps made the arrival of something big apparent. The ACE arrived in the large central hall whose ceiling was high enough to fly in. The man in the suit fired of a shot at the ceiling and watched with glee as men below fled the scene. The main pool connected the Sea water to inside the base, it's what they used to launch their probes and conduct their dives some of the men were scrapping together Scuba Tanks and breathers and making a run for the pool. The base had a rule, No weapons inside the Sanctum.

"I am God's will" he told himself as he revelled through his bloodied mask that he had worn again.

The destructive mayhem continued for a few minutes till he caught sight of Arjun and Vivek. When the both of them saw that the man's attention was on them. They couldn't help but cower. He made his steps deliberately slow and forceful. The idea of him inspiring terror in their hearts gave him pleasure. He was moving closer to them, as the lift arrived. Just in the nick of time, they were able to climb in and close the doors. The lift ride back up was slow and uncomfortable. Also the fear that the masked would do something weighed on them. As Vivek and Arjun came back on top the watched the Sea right beside them and within seconds, out of the sea jumped out the masked man. He had taken another route to the top.

"I am not going to make Grand speeches, but I am going to take over this base for now, till the time some nice people arrive and take me away. So, who wants to tell me, which one of you is in charge of communications?

Arjun immediately noticed an open panel on the back of the suit, as the masked man he turned to talk to everyone.

"I promise nobody would be harmed. Except for those two fuckers right there! Bring them to me!

Vivek and Arjun made their way across the band of confused and scared tailors.

"You punched my face! You made me ugly! Now maybe God is telling me to be a bit more humble but I don't like it as much, so I am going to do to you. What you did to me."

"Wait! There is something that you don't know about the suit."

"What's that?"

"The power will always show 50% or below and you will run out of power until it is calibrated from the back. It's a safety feature to ensure that the suit can't be used single handedly. Only I know the correct sequence now since you killed the other guy by dropping the ceiling on his head.

"OH, and what do you want in return?"

"Spare me and my friends. Take the suit. Go ahead. I don't care."

The HUD was flashing 49% and he needed to have the suit at full power, he didn't have choice but he also knew that these two were cunning and would turn on him any moment.

"Let's do a fair deal, Vivek, come here. Vivek stands in front of me and if my power goes down instead of up, I kill him, Fair deal?"

"Fair deal!"

Arjun climbed on the back of the ACE and accessed the open panel. He looked perplexed and started the procedure. Vivek stood right in front of him and waited for the result. In an instant and without warning, the Suit shut down. The masked man's hands dropped as the suit powered down.

"50% you could have done all that you wanted in 50% but no! I must have a hundred, you must be a joy with your cell phone, always hunting for a charge" Arjun smiled as he climbed down.

"Out of all the ways, you could have gone; you chose the most anticlimactic way to go. You really are dumb but how did you escape?"

"We will beat that out of him."

"Where is Brar when you need him?"

A shot was fired from the back, straight into the man's head. It was Brar, making sure that the secret would die with him. Poseidon couldn't believe it, he shouted in anger!

"What have you done??!!"

"Only what was necessary."

"There is something else going on here"

"Care to elaborate?"

"Not just yet but you can bet that I will dig to the bottom Hades."

"Do what you must; I have a plane to catch back to my base."

Brar nonchalantly walked towards the airfield while Apollo looked back at them, nodded at Vivek and Arjun before joining Brar on his way back,

"Son, I need that suit, you are going in it very soon" Brar said to Apollo as the Military Transport Aircraft closed its doors.

Poseidon looked on as his base now seemed to be in dire need of rebuilding, just 10 minutes in the sea ACE had caused so much damage. he came ahead and thanked Vivek and Arjun for their quick thinking and for saving the skin of everyone on the base; he developed his suspicions about Brar that he would follow. Before going away Vivek asked him the question about where they were. Poseidon smiled and said.

"Hasn't anybody told you? This is the Andaman's. Be around here for a while; get yourself cleaned up the medical team. They should be arriving shortly

"Hey Vivek, it's been really nice knowing you. Thanks for everything"

"I am just going to sit on that beach for a while. Plenty of time for talks later"

He went down and sat in the sand, Arun was already there, trying to divert his mind from the whole couple of days. Vivek took this opportunity to find Riya in the crowd slowly crept up behind her.

"Hey beautiful"

"Hi"

"So, now we can't see any snow leopards, how about we go see some fish"

"Vivek, wait, I have to tell you something."

"What? Can't it wait? Look at the weather, look at the scene, look at me." Vivek said as he repeated Riya's line from before

"Vivek, we can't be together, at least not now"

"What?????"

"This whole experience, its taught me more about who I am and what I want to be. It's showed me a side of myself that I never knew before. It's showed me how much I need to change. It's also showed me how good you are and how... how rotten I am inside"

"There is nothing rotten in you Riya, come on"

"No, there is, and you can't see it and that's also why you are so good. Every time I will see you, I will see what you did for me and that will remind me about how little I was willing to do for you, and it's going to kill me inside."

"Hey, look I don't care. We can see this through, we can work on this!"

"I have to go, I am sorry." Riya parted with tears running down her cheek.

Vivek stood there like a porcelain doll, too stunned to reply and too shocked to close his mouth, when he did finally come to realise the full extent of the moment, he gave up and went back to the sandy beach where Arun and Arjun were already sitting under the shade of a bent coconut tree. He saw Riya being hugged by Rohan who looked at him and let out a wide smile.

"Bastard"

He picked up Sea shell in the sand and fiddled with it. There was a silence for 2 minutes.

"She dumped you didn't she?" Arun said

"No, No, she just needs a little time, you know to process all this, everything that's happened"

"She dumped you."

"No she didn't dump me"

"Kind of sounded like she dumped you dude." Arjun also joined in.

"Yeah, she dumped me." Vivek replied still fiddling with the sea shell making a face.

"You and Women! What's the matter with you?"

Vivek remained silent and looked at the ocean ahead.

"Beers back at my place?" Arun inquired.

"You bet buddy."

"Hey Machine Guy, you are invited too, I don't know if you live in Mumbai or not"

"Thanks,"

Vivek remembered his 1st rule as he looked out to the open sea. Women more than circumstance will make you do stupid things. He could have just said not to the Ladakh trip. He was now in debt, was almost killed several times over, mounted a heroic effort to rescue the woman he loved and in the end, after all he did, he didn't even get the girl.

"Hello, we need to verify that you are all safe and ok," came the voice from behind. The voice was soft and lovely, the person who the voice belonged to, lovelier.

"Great, can you tell me your name?"

"Vivek Sharma"

"Hello Vivek, I am Sub Lieutenant Deshmukh, I be running some checks on all of you to make sure that you guys are fine, is that ok? "

She looked at Vivek and asked him to follow her finger, his attention was elsewhere.

"I am going to check your heartbeat ok Vivek?" Vivek simply nodded in agreement. She put on her stethoscope and checked his heartbeat.
"

"Heartbeat's a little irregular, let's get you checked up properly, Can you walk? We will just go and lie down in the shade there and we will take your Blood Pressure"

"OK", Vivek said as he grinned like an idiot.

Rule number 2- You will inevitably repeat the whole thing with another woman.

The End

Vivek and Arjun will return

ABOUT THE AUTHOR

Vikram lives in Mumbai and operates his company called Beyond Earth. He also teaches photography and loves to travel the Sahyadris whenever possible. This is his first book. He can be reached on author.vikramvirulkar@gmail.com